# The Merger Mogul
By Donna Every

Review.com
Life in LA.com
3·16·13

1

*New York Times September 18, 2008*
*Caveat Emptor! Let the buyer beware.*

*Commenting on the collapse of Shellbury Investments after its merger with Offshore Savings and Loans, the Merger Mogul, Daniel Tennant, CEO of Tennant Consulting said: "People don't usually go into marriage expecting to get divorced, but divorce happens. That's why they should protect themselves with a prenupt. In the world of M&As there are no prenupts and no guarantees. When I'm the consultant on a merger I do everything to make sure that the fit is right and I try to leave no stone unturned in the due diligence, but no deal is perfect and we have little control over what happens afterwards. Caveat Emptor!"*

*Shellbury Investments was the client of Barton Phillips, a merger consultant who has been around since the boom days of M&As...*

Daniel Tennant put down the New York Times as his intercom buzzed.

"Barton Phillips for you on Line one and he doesn't sound too pleased," advised Margaret Bryce, his Personal Assistant.

"Great! Perhaps next time you might want to check if I'm available to take the call then," said Daniel caustically.

"Might as well take the medicine now," said Margaret who had read the article in the office copy of the Times and therefore had an idea of what was about to hit the fan.

Daniel pressed Line one. "Barton. What can I do for you?" he asked cordially.

"You can stop trying to damage my reputation to start with," replied Barton hotly. "You know as well as I do that a lot of mergers fail and through no fault of the consultant."

"I totally agree. That's why I said the buyer should beware. I meant of the target, Barton, not the consultant. How could that be damaging to your reputation? Is there anything else I can help you with? Would you like some advice on a more thorough approach to your due diligence?"

"That's pretty libelous, Tennant. You're insinuating that my client's merger failed because of poor due diligence on my part. If that's your strategy to get clients, you'd better find another one or you'll be hearing from my lawyer!" With that Barton Phillips slammed down the phone.

Great start to the day but not surprising, thought Daniel, looking out of the glass front of his office at the Manhattan skyline. The onset of the recession meant that M&As were beginning to decline, so the merger consultants were beginning to jostle for position to get the choicest morsels before only the carcass was left. If he was totally honest with himself, he was just like the rest of them. As long as the mergers kept coming he was happy. His job was to put them together. If they couldn't stay together afterwards that was not his concern. Everyone knew that the ones who benefitted most from mergers and acquisitions were the consultants.

He'd started his business in 2000, one of the best years for M&As but the next two years saw a slump in the market. Thankfully, he'd made some good money in that first year and with his overheads still fairly low, he was able to hold on until things started to improve. He had worked hard to get where he was, to earn the reputation as 'The Merger Mogul' and the lifestyle that went with it, and he'd be damned if he was going to sit by and watch his company shrink with the market.

"In here now, **Margaret**!" He ordered through the intercom.

Margaret Bryce was in the office in less than a minute. After working with Daniel since the start of Tennant Consulting eight years ago, she knew all of his moods. It would be an understatement to say that this was not a good one. Perching on one of the chairs opposite his massive oak desk she waited, with her pen poised above her notepad, pretending to be oblivious to the tension in his office. His thick black hair looked as if he'd been running his hands through it and his navy blue eyes lacked warmth.

"Since when do you send me calls without screening them, Margaret? You know me well enough to realize that I don't take *medicine* unless I absolutely have to." Daniel began to rub his temples at the beginning of yet another headache. He'd been getting them quite frequently and they were beginning to irritate him.

"Sorry boss, but you must admit that comment was kind of harsh, even for you." She had no qualms about speaking her mind to Daniel.

"Reality is harsh! That's why mergers don't always work out – the plans often don't take reality into account. Due diligence is a major factor! And it's still not foolproof. It's like a marriage in more ways than one. That's why I prefer to stay single. Less messy!" he added cynically.

"For someone who thrives on mergers, you're awfully cynical about a merger in your own life," she replied.

"I have no problem with personal mergers as long as they're temporary. It's just marriage that I'm staying clear of. Now is everything set for the retreat tomorrow?"

Daniel and his consulting team were taking the day off, checking into a spa resort where they were having a spa treatment and then spending the rest of the day brainstorming about how to take the company forward, in light of the changes in the Mergers & Acquisitions market. They had just lost a huge merger which was stopped because of the antitrust laws and that had been a big blow. They needed some new consulting services to keep the business thriving and they needed them soon.

"Of course!" said Margaret. "I've arranged for the team to have an early check in at 10.00 a.m. and the spa treatments begin at 11.00. Everyone has a room booked so that they can settle in before the treatment and the brainstorming session. Since it's Friday, I've arranged for you all to stay overnight and check out on Saturday morning rather than fight the traffic. OK? I've sent the itinerary to everyone."

"This is going to cost a bomb! We'd better come up with some ideas to pay the bill," joked Daniel drily. "To tell the truth, I'm looking forward to the break. I'm tired, but my juices will start flowing once I've had a good massage and relax a bit. Which reminds me, did you book The Bridge Café for my date with Angela Pierce tonight?

"Yes, of course. Do you want me to reschedule that? You'll probably need to get to bed at a decent hour to get an early start tomorrow," suggested Margaret.

"Thanks for the advice mother!" mocked Daniel. "But I'm a big boy. I can still do the dinner and be in my bed by 11.00."

"Alone!" suggested Margaret. She wasn't afraid to show her disapproval of her boss' lifestyle.

"That will be all, Margaret," Daniel replied with a smile. Margaret shook her head as she left the office.

Margaret knew him well. Alone would be a rare thing for him. Well, not that rare these days, considering the long hours he had spent working on that merger that the Government put a stop to and, before that, getting disentangled from a relationship that had become a bit too demanding for him. So maybe that was why he was getting these headaches. He'd been looking forward to this date with great anticipation. Unfortunately, his plans would have to wait until after the retreat. Work came first with him.

Women were great, but a profitable company, a healthy stock portfolio and some good real estate investments were even better and definitely harder to come by. Once you acquired the latter, they appreciated with a little maintenance and care. Women, on the other hand, were easier to come by but took a great deal more maintenance and he didn't have the time or inclination to give that right now. His company needed his attention. Angela appeared to be fairly low maintenance and undemanding, but he'd only just met her, so time would tell.

He reached for the phone on his desk. "Margaret, call Angela and confirm the time for dinner and then bring me two pain killers."

Margaret took two Advil from her desk and went to the small kitchenette for a glass of water for Daniel. At 50 years old she was only 15 years older than Daniel but she felt like a mother to him. Although she and her husband Bob had been married for 26 years they'd never been blessed with children of their own. However, over the years, they'd had more children around than she could count. Young people seemed drawn to her and Bob and they'd often had a house full of nieces, nephews or neighbors which gave them both great joy.

She had been surprised when Daniel hired her eight years ago, not that she wasn't more than competent to do the job, but when she met him she thought that he would have gone for a younger and more glamorous PA. Once she got to know him better, she realized that he'd probably been drawn to her as a mother figure, since his own mother had died when he was in law school and she found out recently that he hadn't seen his father in 25 years. At first she thought him quite cold and heartless, in both his business dealings and his brief relationships, but she now recognized it for what it was: a façade to protect himself from being hurt or used.

Over the years their relationship had grown beyond that of employer/employee although, in the office, she respected his position as her boss. She'd cooked more meals for Daniel and had him over to her house more times than she could count. He was the closest thing she'd come to having a son and she was touched when he asked her to be his next of kin in case of any accidents. So she was becoming quite worried with all these headaches he was getting recently and she wished he would go to a doctor, but Daniel was pretty stubborn. She also knew that he didn't forgive easily, so she wasn't looking forward to the volcano that was going to erupt when he found out that she'd been involved in something that would probably mess up his carefully planned life.

2

Daniel and Angela were shown to one of the coveted tables next to the glass front of The Bridge Café, one of New York's finest restaurants, with its spectacular view of downtown Manhattan. The high rises across the river shimmered against the night sky like jewels on black velvet.

The waiter placed their menus in front of them, said he would return shortly to take their drink order, and retreated discreetly.

"This is wonderful," Angela said appreciatively. "It's the first time I've been here but I've heard a lot about it."

"I can certainly testify that it's as good as its reputation," Daniel confirmed.

"And are you as good as your reputation?" asked Angela with a coy smile, returning her gaze to her attractive companion. At six foot two with a trim athletic body and a face that attracted more than one look as they walked through the restaurant, he'd certainly earned his reputation as a ladies' man.

"Which reputation would that be? The Merger Mogul, as the media has taken to calling me?"

"What else would I be talking about?" she replied in a mock innocent voice. "It's been said that your attention to detail is phenomenal and that you do everything in your power to satisfy your clients. I'm wondering if that goes beyond your corporate mergers," she said with a flirtatious smile.

Their waiter discreetly arrived at their table before he could respond and took their order of Tanqueray and tonic with lime for Daniel and a frozen margarita for Angela.

"Well I try to be consistent in everything I do," smiled Daniel after the waiter left. He was enjoying this verbal foreplay. He liked women who knew what they wanted and Angela was making it plain what she wanted. It was a pity that he couldn't accommodate her tonight. He had a long day ahead of him tomorrow.

"Now what shall we have?" asked Daniel.

"I already know what I want," said Angela picking up her menu, "but let's see, what shall I have to eat?"

Subtlety wasn't her strong point but what the heck; life was too short not to go after what you wanted when you wanted it. Daniel smiled as he picked up his own menu and perused it. "The Bridge Café Oysters are great to start and so is the Taylor Bay Scallop Ceviche. In fact I've never had anything that I didn't enjoy."

"So you come here often," Angela stated.

"About once a month, I'd say." He'd brought many women here and it was a good thing that the Maitre D' was so well trained because he never batted an eyelid when Daniel came in with someone new.

"So that's how you get the best table!" said Angela.

"That's why we work so hard, isn't it? So that we can have the best." That was what drove Daniel. His story wasn't so different from thousands of others. His father had left home when he was ten years old and had never looked back. His mother had struggled to raise him on her meager salary and he had spent most of his life never having enough.

Fortunately, he was bright and determined so he'd studied hard and got a scholarship to go to college. A student loan and part-time jobs got him through law school and he put everything into his first job, learning all that he could about mergers and acquisitions and doing an MBA at night. He soon earned a reputation as one of the sharpest consultants in the firm, which helped when he left three years later to start Tennant Consulting. Along the way he made a vow that he would never lack for anything again and that he would always enjoy the best that life had to offer, no matter the cost.

The waiter brought their drinks and took their dinner order.

"I'm afraid I won't be able to stay as long as I'd like because tomorrow my team and I are having a brainstorming retreat outside of the city and I need to head out early. I have to go home and throw some things into a bag."

Angela's red lips pouted. "That's too bad," she said licking the salt from the rim of her glass, "I was looking forward to inviting you to my place for coffee. I make a mean cappuccino."

Daniel groaned silently and said: "I'm afraid I'll have to take a rain check."

"Perhaps I can cook dinner for you on Saturday night," she suggested.

"That sounds great," said Daniel, feeling his body stir in anticipation.

"What do you like to eat?" Angela asked.

"Oh, I'm easy. I like all kinds of food and I'll try anything at least once."

"Good. I should be able to cook something that you'll enjoy then."

"Oh, I'm sure you will," said Daniel. "So how's work going? Any breakthrough for that new client you told me about?" Daniel changed the subject.

Angela worked with a small Public Relations firm and focused on their Print Media Campaigns. In fact, that's how they met. Her firm had been hired by one of his merger clients to deal with their PR after the merger and she'd introduced herself to him at a cocktail party they'd held just over a week ago to celebrate the completion of the merger. He'd immediately been attracted to her. She was his usual type – a beautiful brunette with a cleavage that beckoned and it was a bonus that she could actually carry on an intelligent conversation. They'd chatted a bit at the party about her work and he could tell that she obviously loved her job. She had confided that she wanted to start her own PR firm some day. He wondered if she saw him as a potential financier. It wouldn't be the first time.

"Work is great," she said with enthusiasm, as the waiter brought their appetizers. "My client, Jenny, is finally beginning to get noticed by the media. One of her articles was just seen by a talk show host at a TV station in her city last week and he wants to interview her on his show. I'm really excited for her."

"That's great news! Do you want to try my oysters?" asked Daniel holding out a tempting morsel on his fork. Angela leaned forward, showing an amount of cleavage that was even more tempting. Daniel's eyes drifted downwards to take in the abundant view and then moved back up to see her lips close around his fork, holding it in her mouth for just a few seconds, closing her eyes in bliss.

"Delicious!" she sighed appreciatively.

Daniel shifted uncomfortably in his chair and for a moment contemplated being late for his retreat. He didn't believe in wasting time so he was ready to take things to the next level but, unfortunately, it wouldn't be tonight. Besides, Saturday wasn't that far away. Delayed gratification was good for the soul or was it confession that was good for the soul? Not for the body but probably for the soul, if he believed that sort of thing. He could delay for two nights. Anticipation was half the pleasure and he was pretty sure this merger would be pure pleasure. He turned his attention back to his dinner and his date. Until Saturday....

3

"Umm, good," groaned Daniel in pleasure as a pair of strong feminine hands manipulated the tense muscles in his shoulders. They drifted down to his lower back, kneading his muscles on the way down and continued their probing and soothing for another fifteen minutes. Daniel was practically asleep by this time.

"You were really tense," the masseuse told him. "Spend fifteen minutes in the sauna and then take a cold plunge in the pool – you'll feel wonderful."

"I feel wonderful already, thanks to you,' said Daniel, reluctantly getting up from the massage table. He wrapped the towel around his slim hips and headed to the sauna.

The team was scheduled to get together, in about an hour, to start their session. He hoped he wouldn't be asleep by then since his body felt like limp spaghetti. He definitely needed that cold plunge to wake him up.

"Ok team, I hope you enjoyed the massage and sauna as much as I did." There were murmurs of appreciation all around. Daniel sat with his team of consultants in a conference room they'd rented for this purpose.

There was Bryan Hardt who had been to law school with him and was one of his few real friends, Ian Bane who was an investment banker, Claire Morgan, an MBA with a specialty in Finance, Benjamin Kreiger, who was a tax specialist and Harold Kellerman, an accountant. All except Ben had been with him for the last four years, when he had to expand the business to handle the work that started flooding his office. Ben joined the group earlier in the year, so this was his first retreat.

They were a good team – young, bright, ambitious and willing to think outside the box. He paid them well and they were loyal to the company, at least as loyal as most employees could be expected to be these days. Most of them, like him, were married to their work and that's the way he liked it. The only exception was Harold who had been married for about ten years.

"As you all know, the M&A market has started to slow down again which tends to happen with a recession. In addition to that the numbers show that a third of the mergers in the past have failed outright (like Shellbury) and almost as many haven't lived up to their objectives. Bottom line is we need to come up with some new services for the business so that we won't be so exposed. We've got a lot more overheads than when I started out eight years ago so we need some more baskets to put our eggs in, so to speak. Any suggestions?" asked Daniel.

"Perhaps the best place to start is with what we already have," suggested Claire. "We can take an inventory of what skills we have in-house and how we can use them differently."

"That's what I was thinking as well," agreed Daniel. "Then we can determine if we need to bring someone on board to make up our deficiency. That person doesn't have to be a permanent part of the team either; we can buy in the skills if we need them."

"We should probably look at our client list and the contacts we've got at our clients and what we know about them since their merger," offered Bryan.

"Good idea. Claire, can you be the scribe? Who's going to transcribe this and put it in some sort of order?"

"Harold!" Everyone else said. They knew their strengths and weaknesses and that was Harold's strength. He nodded in agreement.

After they'd been at it for about two hours, Daniel said: "OK! We created an inventory of our skills, listed our clients and the main contacts in their businesses and now we need to find out which ones are having post merger issues by talking with them, figure out what's causing the issues and how we can help them and ourselves at the same time. Have you got all that Claire?"

"Yeah, in hieroglyphics. Harold, I may have to translate some of this stuff for you. My arms are aching. Is this a good time for a coffee break, boss?"

"Yes. There should be a coffee break set up just outside the door. Let's come back together in 20 minutes."

Two hours later, Daniel let himself into his room. His body was still relaxed from the massage but he was mentally exhausted. They had identified some of the issues that they thought could be the cause of post merger problems, but they hadn't been able to come up with possible strategies to fix them yet. In any case, that would depend on what they found by talking to their clients. His head was now aching again. He had asked the front desk to call him in a couple of hours so that he could get ready for dinner with the team, so he kicked off his shoes, dropped across the king-size bed and was asleep in minutes.

The sound of the telephone woke him. He groped for the offending instrument and dragged it to his ear, growling "Hello!"

"Mr. Tennant this is your wake-up call," said a cheerful voice on the other end.

"Thanks," he muttered and hung up. He sat on the side of the bed, rubbed his hands over his face, felt his day-old stubble and headed for the bathroom. Twenty minutes later, freshly shaved and feeling refreshed he was dressed and heading downstairs to the restaurant where the group was meeting for dinner.

"Here boss!" waved Ben from across the room. He looked refreshed, excited and full of youthful enthusiasm.

Daniel made his way to the table set for six, followed by several pairs of female eyes, and sat down.

"Hi, Ben. You're early. Did you manage to grab some sleep?"

"Nah, I worked out in the gym and then went for a swim."

"Oh, to have half of your energy! What did you think of the retreat?" asked Daniel.

"It was great! I really enjoyed the way everyone tossed out ideas and no idea was considered too stupid, even my suggestions, though I'm the new kid on the block. And I like the fact that we all bring different skills to the business so that we have a good mix of possible services we can offer."

19

"That was my thought when I started to expand the company. We just need to figure out how to fix the problems in the merged companies and we'll be smiling all the way to the bank."

The rest of the team joined them and they spent the next couple of hours enjoying a good meal and talking about what they needed to do when they got back to the office the following week.

"I'll get my part done by Tuesday and e-mail it to everyone," said Harold.

"Thanks Harold. Then we can begin to set up meetings with our clients and see what their issues are and what services we can offer them," said Daniel. "Bryan, your idea to focus on our existing clients first makes good sense, since we already have relationships with them and know their business. I'm glad we have this balance in the team because my tendency is always to be looking for newer and greener pastures rather than grazing old grass, excuse the bad pun."

"Yeah, we know," joked Claire, referring to Daniel's short term relationships with various women. They all laughed as Daniel rolled his eyes and tossed back his gin and tonic.

"What are you doing for the rest of the weekend, Dan?" asked Bryan. "I can't believe you let Margaret book you here with us for company on a Friday night."

"Margaret is hoping to reform me," said Daniel, "so I let her have her way tonight since I didn't feel like fighting through the weekend traffic either. I'll use the time to rest for a date I have tomorrow night."

It was Claire's turn to roll her eyes. "One day, boss, you're going to fall hard for someone and you'll be running to the altar to create your own merger without even having a prenupt and Bryan will be running behind you waving one shouting: Daniel, you forgot this!" Everyone was in stitches at the visual Claire described, especially since Bryan, being a lawyer, was always focused on having all the i's dotted and the t's crossed before they did anything.

"The day that happens you'll know I've lost it," replied Daniel cynically, "so just call the nearest Psych ward to come and pick me up."

"Don't underestimate the power of love!" Claire said, claiming the last word.

The power of love, Daniel thought remembering Claire's words as he turned off the Art Deco bedside lamp next to his king-size bed. Love would never have power over him. According to Maslow's hierarchy of needs, which he remembered studying at university, once you had food, shelter and sex you were off to a good start. He made sure that he had the best of the first two and plenty of the third so he was doing OK. He couldn't remember all the other levels but he was pretty sure that he'd covered all of them. After all he was successful and had a great life; a luxurious penthouse apartment, a successful business and his choice of beautiful and willing women. What else did he need?

4

Saturday night at eight o'clock sharp found Daniel stepping off the elevator on Angela's floor. He found Apt. 9, rang the bell and waited for a few seconds for Angela to open the door.

"Well hello," he drawled as she opened the door.

"Hello yourself." She stood to one side and said, "Come in. Welcome to my humble abode."

Daniel offered the bouquet of flowers and the box of Belgian chocolates he held in his hands and touched his lips to the corner of her mouth as he entered the apartment.

"These are beautiful, thank you. And I love chocolates."

"*You* are beautiful," Daniel said. "I like your dress."

That wasn't surprising since Angela had chosen it strategically. It was soft and flowing with a halter top and a scandalous neckline. It was on the dressy side for a dinner at home, but it certainly whet Daniel's appetite, as it was meant to.

"Thank you, sir," said Angela coquettishly as she led him to the sitting room which was lit by vanilla scented candles on the coffee table and on two floating shelves. The room was small compared to the living room in his penthouse apartment, but tastefully furnished in shades of taupe with turquoise accents. The whole atmosphere shouted "Seduction!" which was just fine by Daniel. His body stirred in anticipation.

"Can I get you a Tanqueray and tonic before dinner?" offered Angela, as Daniel sank into the couch and leaned back against the well-padded arm so that he could see her as she walked to the kitchen.

"That sounds great," he replied watching the sway of her hips as she walked and her dark hair bouncing against her bare back.

"How did the retreat go?" Angela asked as she entered the small kitchen. He could see her through the open partition as she got glasses, ice and poured the drinks; a gin and tonic for him and water for her.

"It was good – very productive. We came up with some ideas that I hope will take the company to the next level," said Daniel. "I also got some good rest so I really should thank Margaret for booking us overnight."

"I shall have to thank her as well," smiled Angela as she handed Daniel his drink and joined him on the couch.

"You're not drinking?" asked Daniel.

"I want to keep a clear head so that I don't ruin the food," smiled Angela "but I'll have some wine with dinner."

She raised her glass and said: "To the next level."

"To the next level," he repeated and gently knocked his glass against hers. He didn't have to figure out if she was referring to his company or to them because as soon as they took a sip, she put down her glass and leaned towards him, her body pressing against his chest and resting one hand on his firm thigh. The muscles clenched under her fingers as she nuzzled his lips with hers, tasting the gin and tonic he had just sipped.

"Yum," she murmured, "Gin and tonic never tasted so good. I need another taste."

He smiled and complied, letting her have her way. It was her apartment and her show and he was willing to be the supporting actor, to a point. Daniel buried his hands in her vibrant hair, holding her head in place as he shared the taste of his gin and tonic and then traced the contours of her back which was left bare by the halter top, feeling her shudder as he did so.

Riiinnng! The bell for the oven sounded, jolting them back to reality.

"Sounds like dinner is ready," whispered Daniel.

"That's the main course," replied Angela, "but I'm enjoying the appetizer." She reluctantly pulled back. "I'd better take it out before it gets ruined."

Daniel picked up his drink and finished it before the ice watered it down too much. "Need any help?" Not that he really knew his way around a kitchen.

"No thanks, I've got everything under control," replied Angela. She pulled a pan out of the oven and placed it on top of the stove. She took an interesting looking salad out of the fridge and put it on the bar as Daniel sauntered over. Next she took two wide-mouth cocktail glasses with shrimp hanging around the rims from the fridge and finally a bottle of homemade salad dressing.

"Would you like some wine with dinner? I've got this wonderful Pinot Grigio that will go great with the shrimp and salad," she said waving the bottle.

"Sounds good," said Daniel. "Here, I'll open it for you."

He expertly uncorked the bottle and poured generous amounts of wine into the oversized glasses on the bar.

"Bon appétit," she said as they clinked glasses for a second time that night.

"Mm, good wine," approved Daniel. He leaned towards Angela and sipped at her lips. "Even better," he said stroking her lips apart. She was breathing a bit faster when he pulled back a few minutes later.

"We'd better eat or we'll never make it to the main course, far less dessert," suggested Angela.

They sat beside each other at the small bar and sampled their starters. "This is delicious," said Daniel as he tasted the salad with her homemade dressing. 'You're obviously a woman of many talents. I'm looking forward to experiencing some of the others."

She smiled seductively and said: "Ditto."

The appetizers were followed by the main course of chicken breasts stuffed with chopped mushrooms, herbs and cheeses. They were tender and perfectly cooked and accompanied by crisp vegetables and scalloped potatoes.

"This is as good as the food at The Bridge Café," complimented Daniel.

"Thank you, sir. I've done a few gourmet cooking classes and I love to cook," smiled Angela, obviously pleased. Daniel refilled their glasses.

"And now for dessert," said Angela as they finished their meal. She took a plate from the fridge. "I made one plate for us to share – strawberries dipped in dark chocolate."

"Mm, my favorite," said Daniel, "How did you know?"

"Feminine intuition," said Angela as she led the way to the couch with the plate of strawberries. "Actually, I asked Margaret yesterday," she confessed. Daniel followed with the bottle of wine and remarked: "Thorough too!"

Daniel leaned back against the couch while Angela kicked off her shoes and draped herself across his lap, with one hand free to reach the strawberries. "I'll feed you," she offered.

She popped a small firm chocolate covered strawberry into his mouth. He closed his eyes and savored it and then held her thumb and forefinger and slowly sucked the melting chocolate from them, starting an ache deep inside her.

"Umm," she moaned. "Let's eat the rest later."

"I agree," said Daniel huskily as he picked her up. "Where's your room?"

5

Margaret looked up as Daniel pushed open the glass door with Tennant Consulting etched on it. He smiled at the receptionist and waved cheerfully to the staff as he passed their cubicles. He was obviously in a good mood.

"Good morning, Margaret!" he said with a broad smile that was rare for him at that time of the morning or, truth be told, any time of the day.

"Good morning," Margaret replied looking him up and down cautiously. "Who are you and what have you done with my boss?"

Daniel laughed. "Really Marg, surely I'm not as bad as all that!"

"I plead the fifth. You look like the cat that ate the canary," she commented.

"Or something!" he replied with another smile, heading to his office.

Margaret rolled her eyes. He was acting like a schoolboy! "I take it your date with Angela went well."

"It was just what the doctor ordered," he said as he entered his office and closed the door. He turned on his computer and his wall-mounted TV which was always tuned to one of the business channels. While the computer was booting up he checked his Blackberry for appointments. Good, nothing until 10.30. He picked up the copy of the NY Times that Margaret had left on his desk and scanned the financial pages. No earth shattering news today. At least he hadn't made any comments to offend anyone. Not that he lost any sleep over offending people.

He was just turning back to his computer when his Blackberry rang. The caller was identified as Angela Pierce.

"Good morning, Angel," drawled Daniel on making the connection.

"Hi, Daniel. Saturday night was amazing! I spent most of yesterday in bed recovering and I'm finding it very hard to concentrate on my work today," she sighed.

Daniel laughed huskily. He didn't have that problem. Work came first with him. "Do you want to go to a show tonight? I have some comp tickets here on my desk for Phantom of the Opera at 9.00. I know you've probably seen it already."

"No problem. I haven't seen it recently and never with you. Shall I meet you there?"

"No I can pick you up around 7.30. That way I can take you back home."

"Looking forward to it, Mogul," said Angela suggestively.

Daniel smiled, said goodbye and hung up. He was still smiling reminiscently when Margaret came in with his coffee and a serious look on her face.

"Don't say it, Margaret," he cautioned.

"Don't say what? I was not going to comment on your empty, self-gratifying love life, although love has nothing to do with it…"

"Au contraire, my love life is not self-gratifying," interrupted Daniel, "Angela was very gratified."

Margaret continued as if he hadn't spoken. "I was going to say that there's someone in reception to see you."

"Who is it?" asked Daniel "I'm not expecting anyone until 10.30."

Margaret paused and answered carefully. "It's your father."

"My father?" exclaimed Daniel. "You must be mistaken Margaret. I don't have a father."

"Daniel, denying it doesn't make it less true. Besides you look a lot like him. Daniel he's ill and he really wants to talk with you."

"How do you know he's ill?"

"He called here a couple of months ago and I've been in contact with him since then," she admitted.

"What? You've been talking with him behind my back for months? Et tu Brute?"

Margaret rolled her eyes. "I didn't tell you because I knew that this is exactly how you'd react. Please hear him out Daniel. There're three sides to every story. You should hear his."

"Great! Just what I need - a sick father who I haven't seen in 25 years. What does he want with me now anyway? I'm not Medicare."

Patrick Tennant waited in the reception area outside Daniel's office. He wondered if Daniel would agree to see him. Not that he would blame him if he didn't. After all, he'd walked out of his life twenty-five years ago. Lord knows he'd tried to make a go of it but after he lost his job things just went downhill from there. He and Daniel's mother were tearing each other apart and in the end he left before it got any worse. He figured they were probably better off without him anyway. Over the years he'd drifted around until he found himself in Virginia where he met a woman who changed his life. It was then that he searched for Daniel's mother to ask her for a divorce so that he could marry Roseanne, but found out that she had died. That was about twelve years ago and he'd kept track of Daniel since then. It was so much easier now with the Internet. He was proud of what Daniel had made of himself but he was concerned that he couldn't seem to settle down. He wondered if it had anything to do with his leaving.

When he was diagnosed with colon cancer a year ago, he knew that he wanted to see Daniel before he lost the battle but the chemotherapy left him very ill and he couldn't make the trip to Manhattan. Fortunately, the cancer went into remission a few months ago and he felt strong enough to begin his efforts to contact Daniel. He'd called Tennant Consulting and spoken to Margaret Bryce. It was a difficult call to make but, in the end, Margaret had listened to his story without seeming to judge him and they'd been in contact ever since. It was she who suggested that he should come to Manhattan to see Daniel now that he was fit enough to travel. She thought the office would be the best place because she knew that if he turned up at Daniel's apartment he wouldn't get past the door. He only hoped that she could convince Daniel to see him. After all, he wasn't sure how much time he had left.

Daniel turned his chair to look out at the Manhattan skyline. His heart had started to beat faster and he could feel the anger rising up inside of him. Because of this man his childhood had been pure hell before he left and worse afterwards. He'd prefer not to remember the fights, going to bed hungry, wearing shoes until they had holes, never having enough, having to move from apartment to apartment when his mother couldn't pay the rent.

He really didn't need this. His life was great now. He had everything he wanted. Besides he'd turned out fine without a father in his life for the last 25 years, so what would he want one for now?

"Daniel,' said Margaret softly, "will you see him?"

"Yeah, why not?" replied Daniel offhandedly. "I can spare him a few minutes before I have to prepare for my meeting."

Daniel continued staring out the window, with his fingers drumming on the desk nervously. He caught himself and deliberately stopped the nervous movements. He heard the door open, drew in a deep breath and swung around.

"Hello, Daniel," said the man who had abandoned him more than two decades ago, as if he'd seen him just last week.

Daniel looked him up and down. It was amazing how much they looked alike except that his father was a couple of inches shorter than he was, totally gray and had the haggard look of someone who had lost a lot of weight recently. Daniel gestured to a chair opposite his desk without getting up or offering a greeting in return.

"What can I do for you?" he asked without emotion.

"Thank you for seeing me. I know I don't deserve the time of day from you, but I had to see you again to make peace with you." He paused. "I have colon cancer and the doctors don't have much hope so I'm putting my house in order, so to speak."

Daniel's heart seemed to stop and then started to race again. He told himself that he didn't really care if his father was dying, except as another human being, and he really didn't want to make any "peace". He just wanted to get on with his life and forget about the past.

"I'm sorry to hear about your cancer. Is that why you're here? You need money for some medical treatment?"

"No, Danny Boy. I've had treatment and the cancer is in remission now but I don't know how long it will last. As I said, I just wanted to ask your forgiveness for abandoning you. I couldn't get work, couldn't provide for you and it was destroying me and tearing your mother and I apart so I figured that leaving was the best thing. I know that it was a cop-out but I was young and irresponsible back then. I know things must have been hard for you after I left and I'm sorry for all you suffered."

"You know nothing about how things were for me," replied Daniel angrily. "But you can leave this world in peace." He gestured around his posh office. "As you can see, things turned out just fine. As for forgiveness, that would mean that you hurt me in some way and that's not the case so you don't need my forgiveness."

Daniel stood up and walked to the door, holding it open. "Sorry that you wasted your time dropping by but it really wasn't necessary. In fact, your leaving was probably a blessing in disguise because it made me determined to succeed and, as you can see, I have. So you can go to your grave knowing that you did something right."

His father got slowly to his feet, looked at him sadly and walked to the door.

"Success is more than possessions and position. You'll find that out. I love you, Danny Boy" he whispered as he passed him and left the office.

Daniel closed the door firmly and stood absolutely still. He'd forgotten that his father used to call him Danny Boy. Clamping down on emotions that he had ruthlessly shoved to the bottom of his heart over the years, he once again came to that place where he felt nothing. It was easier that way.

He walked back to his desk and held his head in his hands. It was now throbbing and there was a ringing in his ears. He pressed the intercom and said: "Margaret, reschedule my 10.30 appointment, call Angela and cancel our date for tonight and then bring me two pain killers."

6

Margaret knocked at the door and walked in carrying a glass of water and two tablets.

"This is becoming a habit, Daniel," she said handing him the pain killers. "Would you like me to set up an appointment for you with Dr. Evans? I'm getting concerned with all these headaches you're having. Besides it's been two years since your last annual," she added drily.

"With the amount of crap that I've been dealing with, it's no wonder I've got constant headaches," snapped Daniel.

"You wouldn't be including your father in that, would you?"

"Of course I'm including him! Where does he get off walking back into my life after 25 years and asking me for forgiveness?"

"So did you forgive him?" asked Margaret.

"I told him there was nothing to forgive, because his leaving made me more determined to succeed and I have."

Margaret raised one eyebrow skeptically.

"Well that means you owe him for your success then. Daniel, he flew from Virginia to see you and he's not even that strong. The least you can do is spend some time with him. Meet your stepmother. You'll probably regret it if you don't."

"Regrets are a waste of time and energy! I don't care if I never see him again!"

Margaret looked at him. "I really think you need to forgive him so that you can move on."

"I have moved on Margaret. I'm thirty-five years old, for goodness sake. What do I need a father for? I've got everything I need."

"*Do* you have everything you need, Daniel?" she asked and left the office without waiting for a response.

Daniel turned back to his computer, clicked on his Windows Mail icon and glanced through files on his desk while he waited for the e-mails to be downloaded. He suddenly felt restless and definitely not in the mood for work today. He had his tennis bag in the car; he would drive to the club and see if he could find someone to play with him, or hopefully the pro would be available. He definitely felt the need to hit something hard.

He stopped the mail in the middle of the download, turned off the computer and TV, stuffed the files on his desk into his briefcase and left his office. Maybe he'd have a look at them later.

"I'll be at the tennis club, Margaret," he said as he walked past her.

Margaret stared after him in amazement. Daniel was going to the club during the day to play tennis instead of working? Yeah, right, he had gotten over his father.

"Aagh!" grunted Daniel as he slammed the ball back over the net to the pro. It dropped just outside the base line.

"Fifteen - thirty," said Geoffrey, the pro, as he threw a couple of balls back over to Daniel.

Daniel tossed the ball up and prepared to hit it over the net with power and missed. He felt dizzy and unsteady on his feet. What was going on? The second serve hit the net.

"Fifteen - forty," called Geoffrey.

The next serve was also a fault and while the second one stayed in, it was no challenge for the pro to get back. The pair rallied for several minutes, each blasting the balls back across the net with precision but unable to get the best of the other. Suddenly Geoffrey sent a blistering shot down the line, passing Daniel who didn't even have the chance to move.

"Game, set and match. Late night?" Joked Geoffrey as they shook hands at the net.

"That's probably it," said Daniel distractedly. "Can I buy you a drink?"

"I'll have to take a rain check," said Geoffrey, "I've got another session in 15 minutes."

Daniel headed for the men's changing rooms. The exclusive tennis club was over thirty years old and was located on the East side of Manhattan near some up market neighborhoods and not too far from Daniel's own penthouse apartment. He'd been a member there for about four years and tried to play at least once a week to keep fit.

Fifteen minutes later, Daniel was bathed and refreshed, wearing a clean pair of walking shorts and a polo shirt he had in his tennis bag. He sat at the bar and ordered a gin and tonic. Probably not the best idea after his dizziness earlier, but he needed it.

"Must be a hell of a day to be drinking a gin and tonic at this time," said a sultry voice. He didn't have to turn around to know who it belonged to. It was Pamela Highland's. They'd been together a few times in the past and had a no-strings-attached kind of relationship.

"Hi Pam," he said turning around and taking in her short, way-too-sexy tennis outfit. "It certainly started out that way but I'm feeling better already," he said, his gaze zeroing in on her ample bosom like a laser beam.

"It must be something big to make you leave your first love, work, at this time of the day. Anything I can do to take your mind off your worries?" she asked sliding between him and the next bar stool. "You know my place is ten minutes away. I'd be happy to give you a back massage or anything else you need," she offered, rubbing her hand up and down his back.

A picture of Angela flashed into his mind and he quickly squelched it. After all it wasn't as if they were in a serious relationship; they'd only slept together one night. Then again when was he ever in a serious relationship? Maybe some time with Pamela was what he needed to get his mind off things for a while.

"Sounds tempting," he said sliding off the bar stool into the space that she already occupied, "and I'm too weak to resist right now." Their bodies pressed against each other in the tight space as he leaned around her and put $20 on the bar rather than waste time charging the drink to his account.

"Is that a gun in your pocket or are you just happy to see me?" she said in her best Mae West impression.

"Let's go find out," he said huskily.

Mike, the bar tender shook his gray head as he watched the pair walk off together. It was obvious what was up. Didn't these kids think about AIDS or anything like that?

"Thanks. I needed that," Daniel said just over a couple of hours later as Pamela walked him to the front door of her luxurious apartment complex, no doubt paid for by her rich daddy.

"Anytime," replied Pamela.

He held the back of her head, gave her a quick kiss on her lips and walked to his black Porsche Turbo without looking back. He got in, started the powerful engine and roared away. Pamela had certainly delivered all that she promised and if he'd used her then she used him too so it was really win-win. So why did he feel so empty?

As he waited at a light, he picked up his Blackberry which he'd left in the car and saw six missed calls, three of which were from Angela. Even as he put it back on the passenger seat it began to ring. The caller was identified as Angela Pierce. He groaned. There was no way he wanted to talk to Angela right now. He really didn't feel like explaining himself to her. He let the phone go to voice mail. He'd get Margaret to send round some flowers and he'd do something special with her later in the week.

Daniel walked into his Upper East Side penthouse apartment, dropped his tennis bag on the floor and went to the kitchen to get a beer from the fridge.

"Is someone there?" asked a cautious voice from the direction of the bedrooms.

Oh, no! He'd forgotten that his cleaning lady would be here although the apartment, with its three bedrooms and en suite bathrooms, hardly needed cleaning since most of it was rarely used.

"Hi Clara, it's me," he called.

"Mr. Tennant," she said approaching, "What are you doing home at this time of the day? Are you sick?"

"Some people might think so," he murmured referring to the time he'd spent with Pamela. "No, Clara, I'm fine. You just go back to your cleaning. I'll do a bit of work here instead of going back to the office."

She looked at him skeptically. "OK, I'll try not to disturb you."

The telephone rang and Clara hurried to answer it. "Hello, Daniel Tennant's residence." That would probably be Angela or it could be Margaret. Before he could signal Clara to ask who it was, she was saying: "Yes, he's right here. Hold on." She held out the telephone.

Daniel reluctantly took the phone. "Hello," he said.

"Daniel, what's going on?" It was Angela as he expected. "First of all you make a date with me, then less than an hour later, Margaret calls to tell me it's off and that you've left the office. I've been calling you for the last three hours and you haven't answered your phone or returned my calls. Where have you been? What's going on?"

"Angela, what is this? We had sex this weekend and that gives you the right to know my every move?" he asked defensively.

There was a shocked silence on the other end of the line.

"You're a cold bastard, Daniel Tennant," Angela said after a while. "You should be in Madame Tussaud's. You look real, but you're nothing more than a cold statue." She hung up.

Daniel slowly hung up the phone. Angela was right. He was a cold bastard.

7

Daniel parked his car in the space marked CEO, Tennant Consulting, picked up his briefcase and climbed out. Walking briskly to the basement elevator he got there just as the door was closing. Bryan Hardt was inside the elevator and managed to hold the door for him.

"Thanks, Bryan. Good morning."

"Morning, Daniel. I didn't see you around much yesterday," he commented.

"I took most of the day off to deal with some personal issues."

"Everything all right?" asked Bryan concerned, since he had never heard of Daniel taking the day off for anything.

"Yeah, it's nothing that I can't handle. But thanks for asking."

"Are we still having that planning meeting to discuss the Aspen Bearings merger at 9.30?" asked Bryan.

"Yes. I spent some time looking through the files at home yesterday and I've started listing the legal issues that are going to come up."

"OK."

The elevator stopped at the 29th floor and they got out and headed for the Tennant offices.

"Morning Susan," they both said to the receptionist who was repositioning the sign on her desk that said 'Director of First Impressions'.

"Good morning Daniel, Bryan," replied Susan, looking up with a smile.

They parted ways by Margaret's desk, with Bryan greeting Margaret and then heading down the corridor to his own office.

"Morning, Margaret," said Daniel.

Margaret smiled up at him. "Oh, my boss is back. Good morning boss."

He threw her a half smile and said: "I'd like you to order an expensive bouquet of flowers and have them sent to Angela's office with an 'I'm sorry' card. Also send a smaller bouquet to Pamela Highland with a 'Thank you' card.

Margaret looked curious but only said:"Right away, boss."

He could see that she was dying to say something further so he said, "Keep out of my business, Margaret," softening his words with a hint of a smile, "and just send the flowers."

"I didn't say a word," she protested.

As Daniel was putting together the files for his meeting with the team his phone rang.

"Daniel, it's George Aspen from Aspen Bearings on Line one," Margaret advised him.

What now? wondered Daniel picking up the phone.

"Hi George, I was just about to have a meeting to plan your merger."

"Well about that, Daniel, I'm afraid I've got some bad news.  The Board has decided that this is not a good time to go ahead with the merger.  Things have really begun to slow down and we're going to have to let some people go, so buying that Mexican operation is not an option right now."

'What?" exclaimed Daniel. "We've already signed a contract to do this deal."

"I'm sorry Daniel, but you know that there is an escape clause in there in case the situation with either company changed.  Obviously we'll pay you for the time you've put in to date but we just can't do the deal right now."

"I'll send you my bill," said Daniel disgustedly and hung up. He sat for a few minutes as the news sank in. If he lost any more mergers they were going to have to look at some cutbacks themselves. He pushed back his chair to go and break the bad news to the team.

A few minutes later the team sat in stunned silence. This was the second merger that didn't fly in about three weeks. Things were looking bleak.

"OK, now you realize just how crucial it is that we diversify our practice. The last thing I want to do is let anyone go, so I expect each of you to get on the phone and start calling clients to see how we can help them. If things don't improve we're talking pay cuts!"

They continued to discuss who would tackle which clients and what strategy they would use for the next hour. After the meeting Daniel returned to his office feeling a little more optimistic than when he'd left it. He checked the e-mails that had come in during his meeting, returned some of the phone calls he had received the day before and read some M&A articles online.

His intercom buzzed. "Daniel, it's Scott Lazerby on Line two," said Margaret.

Scott Lazerby was his stockbroker. With a bear market being announced earlier in the year, he didn't expect Scott to have any good news for him. He hadn't had any good news in the last two weeks!

"Hi Scott,' he said. "Am I poor?"

"Not yet," said Scott seriously, "but the market hasn't bottomed out yet. Your financial stocks are down about 35%. And they're likely to fall some more."

"What's that in dollars Scott?" interrupted Daniel.

'We're talking about two and a half million right now. I suggest that you sell now, if we can find buyers. The general stocks like P&G and Johnson and Johnson are keepers. They're good solid companies and will weather the storm and they're good enough for Warren Buffet. The biotech stocks have great potential; some of those were increasing even when the market started going soft, so you should hang on to those."

"This is crazy Scott. I'm losing my shirt here! Let go of everything that even smells like finance as soon as you can."

"OK boss, I'll be in touch."

Daniel hung up and started to drum on his desk with his fingers. He was getting concerned about his stocks. He owned a couple of pieces of real estate in the city and a condo on the beach in Barbados but his stock portfolio was a significant part of his wealth. He was only half joking when he asked Scott if he was poor because that was something he had vowed he would never be again. His thoughts drifted back to the times after his father had left and he began to feel anxious. The ringing of his Blackberry brought him back to reality.

It was Angela. He guessed that the flowers worked.

"Hello, Angela," he said.

"I got your flowers. They're beautiful Daniel."

"Does that mean I'm forgiven for being such a jerk yesterday? I was dealing with some unexpected personal issues and I took it out on you. Sorry." Apologies didn't come easily to him, nor did sharing personal information.

"You're forgiven, but you have to make it up to me," she joked.

"Oh, I've got plans to do just that. How about dinner at my place on Friday night? Pack for the weekend and I'll be your slave for the entire time."

"Umm, "Angela purred. "I can hardly wait."

Daniel finished the conversation and hung up. One issue dealt with. He wished they were all as easy.

The week crawled by and while Daniel managed to make a significant dent in the pile of files on his desk, he was glad it was the weekend. He was really beginning to get worried about the firm's finances, not to mention his own, and he'd noticed that the Receivables were creeping up. Businesses were beginning to feel the effects of the recession already and predictions for next year were pretty dire as well. He hoped he wouldn't have to sell any of his properties to keep the business afloat because it sure as hell wasn't a sellers' market and he'd suffer losses. Was there any silver lining to this dark cloud?

His thoughts went to the weekend ahead and he felt a surge of anticipation at the thought of Angela coming over. He'd hardly call that a silver lining but at least it would take his mind off his financial concerns for a while. That reminded him to buzz Margaret so that she could confirm the time that the caterers were to deliver the dinner to his apartment.

Daniel's doorbell rang promptly at 8 o'clock. He opened it and found Angela standing with an overnight bag in her hand which looked quite small for a weekend visit and wearing a mouthwatering dress in turquoise, which seemed to be her favorite color.

"Hello Angel," Daniel said, missing nothing in his perusal of her.

"I don't feel very angelic tonight," she said.

"Good," said Daniel as he took the bag from her and pulled her into the apartment. Closing the door, he pushed her back against it and began kissing her hungrily.

"I like your welcome," murmured Angela breathlessly after a few minutes.

"Then you'll love your stay," replied Daniel kissing her again.

Angela's stomach growled loudly and she said with embarrassment, "Sorry but I'm starving. I hardly ate at all today. I was so engrossed in a project."

"OK let's get you fed then," said Daniel starting to lead her to the dining room. "Oh, I almost forgot, I have something for you first."

Angela laughed. "Oh I like the sound of that, what is it?"

Daniel went back to the hall table and picked up the little box he'd left there earlier.

"Hope you like them."

She opened the box and peered inside to see a stunning pair of turquoise drop earrings in a platinum setting. "Oh, Daniel, these are beautiful! You didn't have to... but I'm glad you did," she finished with a big smile. She moved closer to the circular mirror over the table and put them in. Daniel came up behind her and trailed his lips from the back of her ear all the way down her neck, taking small bites as he went. She broke out in goose bumps and fell back against him.

"Do you still want to eat first?" he asked. "Your wish is my command."

Pulling his head down, she whispered her wish in his ear. Leaning back against him she could feel the immediate response of his body to her words and felt a thrill of power at the effect she had on him.

"Let's go to your room," she suggested.

"Too far," he murmured, "the couch..." his voice trailed off as he led her to the couch and they fell onto it in a tangle of limbs.

Daniel disentangled himself from Angela and dragged himself from the couch. "I'll go find us something to slip on," he said. His words came out a bit slurred and he wondered at the dizziness he felt. Probably the blood hadn't returned to his head yet. Heading to the bedroom he stumbled a little, shook his head as if to clear it and headed over to the walk-in closet where he found some clothes for him and a robe for Angela.

He pulled on a pair of black track pants and took one of his silk robes for Angela. He turned around and began heading down the hall but a wave of dizziness hit him again followed by a shocking pain on the right side of his face. Then his face felt numb. What the hell...?

He stumbled into the living room and said "Angela, I feel kind of weird, as if I'm having a stroke or something. Call 911," and dropped to the couch holding his head.

Angela jumped up and put her hand on his forehead. "Daniel, you're burning up!"

She looked around in a panic for a telephone and spotted his Blackberry on the coffee table. She grabbed it and punched in the numbers with trembling fingers.

"This is 911, how can I help you?

"Pl..please send an ambulance to Penthouse Apartment 2 at East River Apartments on 59th Street. My friend might be having a stroke. Hurry! Please Hurry!"

8

The paramedics rushed through the doors of the ER which were being held open by two orderlies and ran to the approaching ER team, pushing the trolley with Daniel on it.

"What've we got?" asked a doctor.

"His name is Daniel Tennant; 35 years old. He's complaining of numbness on the right side of his face and has been dizzy. His temperature is $103°$. Pulse is 78 and BP is 120 over 70.

"Mr. Tennant, I'm Dr. Halloway. How are you feeling now?"

"The right side of my face is still numb and I feel as if I'm drooling. Did I have a stroke?" Daniel mumbled.

"We have to run some tests and do some blood work before we'll know anything definite. We may have to take you to radiology for an MRI. Thanks guys," he said to the paramedics, "We'll take it from here," and started to push Daniel down the hall to an examination room.

Angela trailed behind, unsure of what to do. A nurse approached her and said, "Did you come in with that patient?" At her nod she added, "You'll need to go to that lady over there and complete some paper work." She pointed to the Administration booth.

"I don't know him that well," Angela said realizing that she really didn't know very much about Daniel. She didn't know if he had any family, who to contact or anything. What sort of relationship was that? She'd been out with him once, slept with him and still knew almost nothing about him. Daniel wasn't exactly forthcoming with information about himself. It was all so empty. Dragging her thoughts back to the present situation, she wondered who she could contact. Margaret would know. Thankfully she had picked up Daniel's Blackberry. Margaret's number would be in there. What was her surname again? On no, she couldn't remember. She began scrolling through the received calls, seeing her own name a few times and was relieved to see a call from Margaret Bryce. Yes, that was it! Checking through the contacts she found a home number and called it.

The phone rang three times. She hoped Margaret was not in bed already.

"Hello?" It was Margaret's voice.

"Hello, Margaret. It's Angela Pierce. I'm sorry to call you so late but I'm at New York Memorial on 61st Street. It's Daniel. He felt ill when I was at his apartment and asked me to call 911 and the ambulance brought us here."

"What happened?" Margaret asked anxiously.

"Well he went into his room and then he came back and said that he felt weird, that his face felt numb and he was burning up with fever. It was all so sudden!"

"Where did you say you were? I'm coming down right away."

"We're at New York Memorial on 61st Street. I'm supposed to complete some forms but I don't even know who his next of kin is or anything."

"I'm listed as his next of kin, although his father is still alive. I'll do the forms when I get there. Don't worry and thanks for calling me, Angela."

The neurologist and the radiologist looked at the results of the MRI mounted on the wall.

"There's the culprit," said the neurologist. "It's a big one. Acoustic neuroma pressing against the brain stem. He must have been getting some major headaches, but then again headaches can be anything. He's going to need surgery and soon. I'd better go down and break the news to him." He picked up the chart, scanned the information on it and wrote down some notes.

"Daniel Tennant. That name seems familiar," he said.

"He's always in the financial papers and sometimes the tabloids as well. They call him The Merger Mogul.

He's one of those big time merger consultants with a lot of money and a lot of women," shared the radiologist.

"Well The Merger Mogul won't be doing any mergers for a while, business or otherwise."

The neurologist took the elevator back down to the ER and a nurse directed him to the room Daniel was in.

Walking up to the bed he said: "Daniel Tennant? I'm Gabriel Bucknell. I'm a neurologist. I've just gone over the results of your MRI with the radiologist." He paused.  Daniel's heart stopped. He felt like he was at the top of a giant rollercoaster and braced himself for the drop. "You have an acoustic neuroma the size of a golf ball pressing on your brain stem and it's affecting your right facial nerve."

"What's that?" interrupted Daniel.

"It's a tumor on the nerve leading from your inner ear to your brain. These types are usually benign.  You may have noticed some ringing in your ear, headaches or dizziness…"

"A brain tumor?" Daniel repeated incredulously. "It's benign?  Are you sure?"

"As I said, these types usually are and they are operable but because of its position there is a certain degree of risk."

Daniel closed his eyes in disbelief. How was this possible? Only a few hours ago he was enjoying the beginning of what looked to be a great weekend and now he was in the hospital with some doctor telling him unemotionally that he had a brain tumor and he could possibly die in surgery? This was too much!

"Our resident neurosurgeon will be back on Monday and will be able to give you more information about the operation and the likely outcomes. You'll be admitted to a room until then. Is there someone here with you?"

"Yes," Daniel said vaguely, "Angela Pierce. She may be in the waiting room."

The neurologist nodded and left the room to find Angela.

Daniel closed his eyes again. He felt a paralyzing fear come over him. It held him in its grip and refused to let go.

Margaret and her husband, Bob, arrived at the ER waiting area and found Angela sitting on one of the hard, plastic chairs looking rather lost and out of place in her revealing dinner dress. Margaret went over to her, followed by her husband. Although they had spoken on the phone several times they had never met.

"Hello, you must be Angela" said Margaret hugging her. "I'm Margaret and this is my husband, Bob. How's Daniel?"

"I haven't heard anything yet. They took him for an MRI. I started to fill out the forms, but here, you can complete them. I realize that I really don't know Daniel at all," she ended handing over the clip board.

They sat down and Margaret filled in the areas that Angela had left blank. The neurologist walked into the waiting area, looked around and said: "Angela Pierce?"

Angela and Margaret sprang up looking tense. "I'm Angela Pierce," said Angela. "And this is Margaret Bryce, Daniel Tennant's Personal Assistant and she's also listed as his next of kin. Is he going to be all right?"

"Let's sit down. I'm Gabriel Bucknell. I'm a neurologist. I'm afraid that Mr. Tennant has a brain tumor." Both Angela and Margaret gasped. "It's operable and there's a good chance that he should fully recover but there may be some complications."

"Oh no!" said Margaret, her hand going to the throat. "He's been getting these headaches and I told him to let me make an appointment with his doctor, but he kept putting me off because he hates doctors and medicine and that type of thing. Have you told Daniel yet?"

"Yes, I have. Our resident neurosurgeon won't be back until Monday. He'll be able to discuss the surgery more fully with Mr. Tennant. Until then we will be admitting him to a room."

"May we see him now?"

"Yes, of course."

He led Margaret and Angela to the room in the ER where Daniel lay in a bed with his eyes closed. Angela started to cry softly and ran outside. Margaret felt like crying too but she held it in. Daniel was like a son to her and seeing him lying on the bed looking so vulnerable hurt more than she would have thought possible. He could be a pain but she loved him. He had so little love in his life and while on the surface it seemed as if everything was fine, she knew that inside he was really very lonely and empty.

"Please don't let him die," she whispered in prayer. She walked to the side of his bed. "Hi Daniel," she said. She stroked his hair back from his brow which was now normal.

"Margaret? What are you doing here? Where's Angela?" he asked opening his eyes

"She's outside. She's a bit upset to see you like this. She found my number and called me."

"Have you heard?" Daniel asked.

"Yes, Dr. Bucknell told us."

"A brain tumor, Margaret! Why? Why now when I'm finally living the life I've always wanted? Is this some sort of sick joke? I'm not ready to die."

"Only the good die young," she teased gently trying to ease the tension.

"Then I should live to a hundred!" scoffed Daniel. "Their big shot neurosurgeon is supposed to come in on Monday to give me the details. How the hell am I supposed to lie around here for two days without knowing anything?"

"I know that will be hard for you Daniel but you can use the time to do some soul searching. Perhaps someone is trying to get your attention. I'll come and see you tomorrow." Margaret kissed his brow and left quietly.

Daniel lay in the bed with feelings of helplessness, anger and fear washing over him in turn. If someone was trying to get his attention, then they certainly had it.

9

*New York Chronicle*
*Monday September 29, 2008*

*The Merger Mogul, Daniel Tennant, was rushed to hospital on Friday night after what appeared to be a stroke; however this has not been confirmed as yet. Tennant, who is only thirty-five years old, was said to have been accompanied to the hospital by an unknown young lady...*

Daniel flung the newspaper which had been delivered to his room to the bottom of his bed. Was nothing sacred? How did the press find out these things anyway? And where the hell was the top notch neurosurgeon who was supposed to come and see him?

For two days he had lain in this uncomfortable hospital bed, waiting and wondering with his thoughts torturing him. He couldn't concentrate on anything showing on the wall-mounted TV and now his head was beginning to pound again and he felt hot. He pressed the button next to his bed and a nurse appeared in a few minutes.

"Nurse, can you give me something for this headache? And I think I may have a fever. I feel hot," he complained.

She took his temperature with an ear thermometer and noted that it was 101° F.

"You do have a temperature, Mr. Tennant. I'll go get you some pills to bring down the fever and help your headache."

"Thanks."

Daniel was once again left with his thoughts. The neurologist had told him he had a tumor the size of a golf ball in his head! How was that even possible? He didn't know what the risks of removing it were, if he'd ever recover completely or at all. He'd asked Margaret to bring his laptop so that he could do his own research but she'd refused. He felt so helpless and frustrated! He was going crazy just lying here. He was going to check himself out if the surgeon didn't show up soon. In fact he should probably get a second opinion.

Half an hour later the door opened and a tall man with graying hair wearing blue surgical clothes entered the room.

"Mr. Tennant, I'm Luke Wellington, the neurosurgeon here. I've been away and just got back this morning."

"I'm glad to see you. The waiting was driving me crazy!"

"I'm sorry about that.   OK this is what we're dealing with. As you know you've got an acoustic neuroma, which is resting on your brain stem.  It's also impacting your facial nerve which is why you may have felt shooting pains in your face and then numbness.

"There are risks associated with removing the tumor because of the size and position.   We can take two approaches: Try to remove the whole tumor surgically or remove part of it and treat the rest with radiotherapy.  If we remove the whole thing we risk damaging the facial nerve which could result in permanent paralysis of the right side of your face and make your face droop, to put it in layman's terms.  We should be able to get around the facial paralysis by preserving the facial nerve and we will work closely with an ENT surgeon to do that. We would leave the part of the tumor that's resting on the nerve and deal with it afterwards using radiotherapy. Whichever approach we take, you're likely to lose the hearing in your right ear. How do you want us to proceed?"

Daniel closed his eyes.  He couldn't believe this! How did he want them to proceed? What he wanted was to go to sleep and wake up and find that this was all a dream. He could either die in the operation or, if he survived, he could lose the hearing in his right ear and possibly have half his face drooping!   What options were those?

He took a deep breath. "I certainly don't want my face drooping. Leave in part of the tumor and treat it afterwards. How long will the operation take and how long do I have to do the radiotherapy, assuming I survive?"

"Your survival chances are excellent, Mr. Tennant. I've done this operation a number of times successfully. The operation takes about 10 hours. Because of the size of the tumor, we'll need to make an incision in your skull to remove it, so we'll have to shave your hair in that area. The trauma to your brain will cause some swelling but once the swelling goes down we can begin the radiotherapy. That could be anywhere from 25 to 30 treatments. It's usually done from Monday to Friday for five to six weeks. You could be out of commission for three to six months, depending on how quickly your body responds."

"Three to six months!" exclaimed Daniel.

"You'll have to learn to function again," said the neurosurgeon seriously. "In addition to the trauma to your brain, your balance will be affected which may feel like you're on a rocky boat for a while or you may experience dizziness, so you'll need to do exercises to improve your balance. You'll also find that you've lost a lot of your strength, especially after the radiotherapy and you may experience adverse effects from that like nausea, hair loss and dryness in your mouth. I'll make sure you have a brochure so that you'll be aware of the symptoms and side effects that you may experience.

"I've scheduled the operation for Wednesday morning if you're in agreement." Daniel nodded vaguely. "You'll need to sign consent papers before then. I'll see you in surgery."

God! Why was this happening to him? He knew that he wasn't a saint, but there were a lot worse people than him, who were walking around perfectly healthy. Why him? Why now? Was it only a week ago that his father came to see him to make peace, as he put it, before he died? At that time he never considered that he was anywhere near death himself. Maybe that was why this was happening, to show him how it felt to know that death was just around the corner. What he did know, was that he wanted to avoid that particular corner at all costs.

He needed to see his team before surgery to make sure that things would run smoothly in his absence, or worse case scenario, his death. He didn't even want to go there. That just could not happen. He reached for the telephone next to the bed and called Margaret at the office.

"Hi, Margaret. I'm to have the surgery on Wednesday morning so I need to see you and the rest of the team here later today or tomorrow for a quick meeting."

"OK, Daniel. I'll arrange for the team to come tomorrow but I'll see you later."

"Thanks Margaret. Oh and Margaret, say some prayers for me."

"Already on it, Daniel," replied Margaret.

*Next day*

Margaret knocked on Daniel's door, opened it a crack and stuck her head in.

"Ready to see us, Daniel?"

"Yeah Margaret. I've been waiting for you guys."

The team filed into the room feeling kind of awkward to see Daniel lying in bed. It was only a couple of weeks ago that he was leading them in the brainstorming session and he had looked perfectly healthy. It made all of them very aware of their own mortality.

"Hi Boss," they chorused.

"Hi guys, thanks for coming," Daniel said. "Sorry I can't offer all of you chairs so I'll make it quick. I'm sure Margaret has told you about this damned tumor. I'm having the operation tomorrow morning and, assuming I survive it, the surgeon says that I could be out of it for as long as six months.

"Bryan, you're in charge while I'm away. You're already a signatory on the bank account, so that ball is now in your court. Don't let them talk you into giving raises while I'm away," joked Daniel. Everyone laughed to release the tension. "Start to roll out the new stuff that we came up with at the brainstorming session." Bryan nodded. "I've started contacting our clients via e-mail to let them know what's happening and that you're in charge."

Daniel continued, "You're a great team and you've helped to make Tennant Consulting what it is. I hope to see you on the other side of this operation."

Each one came up to the bed to shake Daniel's hand as they left. Claire leaned over and hugged him with tears in her eyes and said: "You come through this, you hear?"

"I plan to," replied Daniel. He couldn't contemplate anything else. They left him with Margaret.

"Bob and I will be here this evening. He's been worried about you," said Margaret. "I'll bring some of your favorite food for dinner."

"Thanks Margaret. What would I do without you?"

"Would you like me to call your father? He's gone back to Virginia but you can speak to him on the phone."

"I really don't have anything to say to him, Margaret and I'd be a hypocrite to call him now and tell him I forgive him because of what's happening with me."

Margaret looked at him sadly and said: "Daniel, you may live to regret this."

"I hope I live to regret it," he joked cynically. "As I said Margaret, regrets are a waste of time."

*Later that evening*

Daniel was sitting in his visitor's chair with his laptop open on his lap. Margaret had relented and brought it when she came earlier; he was catching up on his e-mails and sending out messages to his clients about his situation, and assuring them that they would still be in good hands with Tennant Consulting in his absence.

There was a knock at the door.

"Come in," called Daniel. Bob and Margaret came in carrying a basket.

"Hi, Daniel," greeted Bob. "You look fine. Are you sure that MRI was right?"

"Yeah, hard to believe isn't it? I saw it myself. Kind of amazing that something so big could be in your head and you not know it."

"Margaret tells me the surgery is scheduled for tomorrow morning. We'll both come and see you before you go in."

"You don't need to do that," protested Daniel.

"You're like a son to us, Daniel," added Margaret. "We wouldn't want to be anywhere else. We're praying for you and we know that you're going to come through this."

"I hope so," Daniel replied. "I really hope so."

"I brought your favorite dinner, grilled salmon and risotto" she said changing the subject. "Eat up while it's still warm."

"Is this like the last meal before the execution or rather, the surgery?" joked Daniel.

"I don't know how you can joke about this," scolded Margaret.

"It's either that or completely lose it," he admitted.

10

Daniel lay on his bed with his eyes open. The clock on his bedside table displayed 11.33 pm but he couldn't sleep. Thoughts were swirling around in his head. Thoughts of death. He wondered what it felt like to die. Did you take a breath and then try to take another one but there were no more? Is that when panic set in? Did it all end there or was there really life after death as some people believed? He'd never really thought about it. His own death wasn't something he had given much thought to before because he'd been so busy living and trying to be successful.

His mind took him back over his life, to the struggles he and his mother endured after his dad left. His life could have turned out so differently if his mother had not drummed into him the need to work hard and be successful so that he wouldn't have to ever live like that again. He'd taken her words to heart and worked hard to get where he was today.

He remembered the excitement of winning a scholarship to go to college and the many hours he worked to supplement that money. He remembered the sense of achievement he felt when he graduated from law school. Sorrow overcame him as he thought how his mother had died, before he graduated, and before he'd had the chance to give her all the things that he would have liked to. He smiled as he remembered how rich he felt when he earned his first big pay check (a pittance compared to what he earned now) and the fear, mixed with excitement, he experienced when he took the risk and started Tennant Consulting.

He thought of the women who came so easily as his reputation and wealth grew and even before then. He couldn't even remember all of their names. What did it all mean? Who was it that said "Vanity, vanity, all is vanity?" He couldn't remember but he definitely agreed with that. Where was the meaning in his life? What was it all for? What was the point of pursuing wealth at all costs? Who would he leave it to anyway? Who would care if he died? Maybe Margaret and Bob, but no-one else really. Was this all there was to life?

His head began to ache with all the thoughts and he longed for the oblivion of sleep, although at the same time he wanted to stay awake in case it was the last day of his life.

*Next morning – 9.00 a.m.*

Daniel looked up at the fluorescent lights as he was wheeled to the preparation room. From his position on the trolley he felt out of control and helpless. He'd told Margaret and Bob not to come but now he wished they were here and he could see their familiar faces before he went into surgery.

The trolley stopped just outside the prep room and his eyes left the ceiling to see what the holdup was. Next to the trolley he saw the very faces he'd just wished for a minute ago. He felt a surge of love for these two people. It was an emotion he hadn't felt in a very long time.

"Didn't think that we would let you go under the knife without showing our faces, did you?" asked Bob.

"We'll be praying for you, Daniel," Margaret assured him.

"Thanks you two. I'm glad you ignored me and came anyway." He wanted to tell them that he loved them but the words stuck in his throat.

Before he could get the words out, he was taken into the operating theatre for the surgery which would last the next ten hours, if it didn't end prematurely.

Daniel slowly regained consciousness. He tried to open his eyes but the brightness made him quickly close them again. The first thought that registered in his head was: "I'm alive!" which was quickly followed by a wish for death as the most excruciating pain he had ever felt exploded in his head when he moved it. A surge of nausea overcame him and he opened his eyes again just in time to spot and grab a bowl on the trolley next to his bed and he emptied what little he had in his stomach into it. That movement made him feel like dying.

He eased himself back on the pillow and lay as still as he could. He was afraid to move any part of his body, afraid of the pain that was just waiting to overpower him with even the slightest movement of his head. He willed a nurse to come into the room so that he could ask for something to kill the pain. He cautiously moved his eyes to the side and could see the call button so temptingly close, but the thought of reaching for it was outweighed by the memory of the pain he had felt when he moved his head before. He was trying to decide if he should try to endure the pain in order to get medicine, when he succumbed to the anesthetic that was still in his blood stream and drifted into sleep again.

The next time he woke up he found Margaret and Bob sitting in the visitors' chairs at his bedside flicking through magazines.

"Hi," he croaked, speaking for the first time in nearly twenty-four hours. Their eyes flew to him.

"Hi, Daniel. You're finally awake! How do you feel?" asked Margaret.

"Like someone cut out a piece of my brain," he replied hoarsely. They chuckled softly. He closed his eyes again and said dejectedly, "I can't hear through my right ear."

"I'm sorry, Daniel. Mr. Wellington warned you that would happen but I guess it doesn't make it any easier.

I'll call a nurse to give you something for the pain and maybe a drink of water. At least you're alright." Margaret gently squeezed Daniel's shoulder and left the room to find a nurse.

Alright? He was alive but that was it. He had never felt worse in his life.

The door opened and a pleasant looking nurse came in, followed by Margaret.

"Welcome back, Mr. Tennant," greeted the nurse. "I've brought you some medication for the pain but it may make you feel a bit strange."

"No problem. Anything to kill this pain."

Daniel drank some water first and then swallowed the tablets and prayed that they would start to take effect soon. His head felt like it was in a vice and it hurt so badly that he wanted to die. Considering how bad he had wanted to live that was pretty ironic. He had thought that once he'd had the operation the worst would be over, but now he didn't know how he would get through the next six hours far less the next six months! He felt depression creeping up on him. It wasn't an emotion he was familiar with since he had always taken things in stride and just got on with whatever he needed to do. Now there was nothing he could do. He couldn't speed up his recovery, he couldn't stop his head from hurting, he couldn't hear through his right ear and he couldn't even go to the bathroom by himself! He felt helpless, defeated and in excruciating pain. Maybe death would have been better than this.

Bob saw the look of defeat come over him. "Don't worry, son. You don't have to go through this alone. We're here for you and God is here for you."

"God?" scoffed Daniel. "If he's out there somewhere why should he be here for me? I've never had the time of day for him."

"Because he loves you in spite of that," replied Bob.

"Yeah, OK. I don't want to talk right now." He didn't want to hear about God or anything. He just wanted the unbearable pain in his head to stop.

"OK, we'll go and let you rest some more," said Margaret.

After Bob and Margaret left, Daniel was alone with his thoughts once again. His life had been spared for some reason. Maybe he had some unfinished business to do, but he didn't have a clue what that was. Whatever the reason, he'd been given a second chance. Perhaps it was to use what he would learn from this experience. Already he'd learned that fame and fortune meant nothing when you were staring death in the face. So what was important? What could fill the void that was still a part of him? And for the first time in his life he acknowledged that there was a void. He'd tried to fill it with work, wealth and women but it was still there.

## 11

Daniel's door opened after a brief knock and Luke Wellington walked in.

"Well, Mr. Tennant, you've come through the surgery remarkably well. I know you may not feel like that right now but, although you've lost the hearing in your right ear, the good news is there's no facial paralysis. Your left ear will begin to compensate for the hearing loss and as long as you turn that side to people when they speak, you'll be fine."

"Looks like you did a great job, Mr. Wellington. Thank you."

"You can thank me when we've taken care of the rest of the tumor and you're back on your feet. You'll find that you're going to have to learn how to find your balance again and regain your strength. The hospital has a number of physiotherapists on staff who can help you but that won't be until after you complete your radiotherapy because you probably won't be up to physiotherapy when you're doing that."

"How long do I have to stay here?" asked Daniel. His head still hurt, he felt dizzy and he couldn't even get himself to the bathroom because he was so unstable on his legs. Bob and Margaret had insisted that he come and stay with them until he was well enough to be on his own.

"I'd like to keep you here for a week, make sure you're doing OK before we let you go home. You're to start radiotherapy once the swelling goes down. It will be five days a week for about five or six weeks. As I told you before, you may experience some side effects like nausea, dizziness, that type of thing but we'll treat you with drugs to minimize the effects. You will need someone to drive you to therapy and to keep an eye on you at home. Once you've finished those treatments you can start the physiotherapy which could take up to two months."

Great! For someone who hated to take medicine and to see doctors, he was about to see more of them in the next few months than he had in his entire his life. At least he had a life and for that he should really be grateful.

*A week later*

Daniel lay immobile while radio waves were applied to his head to remove the rest of the tumor. The actual procedure was painless but his whole face and head were covered by a mask made of some kind of plastic which had been molded to fit the shape of his face before he left the hospital. It felt like a vice and was so tight he thought it would crush the rest of his brain. It made him feel claustrophobic and he couldn't wait for the few minutes of radiation to finish before he could get it off. He could relate to the Phantom of the Opera. He had nothing to do but think as he lay there. He couldn't imagine how he was going to endure this for the next six weeks. Wellington had also warned him that he might feel nauseous from the treatments. God, he hoped not. Moving his head around was still agonizing, he couldn't imagine what it would feel like if he was throwing up as well. Was he really supposed to be learning something from this? No answers were forthcoming, but then again, he didn't expect any. He realized that he had little control over what fate threw at him, but it was up to him how he responded. Right there and then he made a vow that this would not defeat him.

*Several hours later*

Daniel tried to remember the vow he had made in the radiation room, as he leaned over the toilet in his bathroom at Margaret's house and heaved the contents of his stomach up. The violent movements made pain explode in his head and drained him of what little energy he had. He washed his mouth and staggered back to his bed, leaning heavily on the walker that he had bought to help him about in these early days.

"Daniel, are you alright?" asked Margaret knocking softly on the door. When he didn't answer she pushed open the door and repeated the question louder. She kept forgetting that he only had hearing in one ear now and he was still adjusting to that.

"No, I'm not alright. I feel sick and weak and I don't know how the hell I'm going to get through these next few weeks."

"The hospital gave me some medicine to help with the nausea. I'll get it for you now. Would you like some broth?"

Daniel groaned at the thought of food. He had little appetite and his mouth tasted metallic anyway.

"That's the last thing I want Margaret. I'll just rest a bit." He hoped she would leave. He appreciated all that Margaret was doing for him but, right now, he just wanted to be left alone.


*Two weeks later*


Daniel ran a comb gently through his hair as he prepared for yet another session of therapy. He stared in horror at the comb which was full of hair and the vanity which was littered with even more strands. He closed his eyes in despair. As if the tiredness and nausea weren't bad enough, his hair was now falling out. He'd read about it but still wasn't prepared for the reality of it. He'd have to ask Bob or Margaret to shave the rest off since he was definitely not going to the salon that he frequented for that. He cleaned up the hair and went to find Margaret.

"Marg, my hair is falling out. I'm going need you or Bob to cut the rest of it short for me. I'm sorry to be such a burden on you two. God, I'm so sick of being sick! Death is beginning to look a whole lot better than this."

"Daniel Tennant, don't let me hear you talking like that. You're not a burden. You have a lot to be thankful for and this won't last forever. You'll get through it. You have a lot of people who are praying for you and who care for you. Angela called again. She wants to see you and so do the folks from the office. I can't keep putting everyone off."

"I really don't feel like seeing anyone right now, Margaret, especially now that my hair is falling out. I look sick. Tell Angela I'll call her when I'm feeling better and let the folks know that I appreciate their cards and good wishes. I don't know Marg, I just don't have the energy or inclination to see anyone and answer questions about how I feel. I just feel empty. My hair falling out is just the last straw. I can't imagine it can get any worse than this."

"Maybe you should see a therapist," suggested Margaret.

"Margaret if I have to see anyone else in the medical profession, that would definitely make me lose it. Don't worry about me. As you said, I'll get through this. I've got through a lot of things in my life. Granted this is the worst, but I've had a lot of preparation."

*Later that evening*

"Daniel," said Margaret knocking softly at his bedroom door. Daniel was lying in bed in the dark. He'd come back from therapy several hours ago and had just crawled into bed after another bout of vomiting.

"What is it Margaret?" His voice was weak and he sounded so low that she hated to add to his depression with the news she just got.

"I'm afraid I have some bad news for you, Daniel," she said softly. "Your father's wife just called. I'm afraid that he lost the battle with the cancer today, Daniel. I'm so sorry."

Daniel froze. Not now! He already felt sick and weak and now this! His father was dead. He remembered how sick he had looked the day he came to see him in his office when he asked for his forgiveness and he hadn't given it. Now he was gone and he would never see him again, never have the chance to say that he forgave him. Regret jack-hammered a path through his heart leaving in its wake a gaping chasm that he felt nothing could ever fill. He remembered telling Margaret caustically that he hoped he lived to regret it. Well he had and he never imagined that it would hurt so bad.

Finally he said weakly: "I can't take anything else Marg. I feel like I'm drowning. I said earlier that things couldn't get any worse, but I was wrong."

*One month later*

The orderly pushed Daniel's chair through doors that were labeled *Physiotherapy Department*. He'd insisted that Margaret leave him at the hospital and come back later. This was to be first therapy session and he wasn't looking forward to it. Having gone through six weeks of radiotherapy he'd had enough of hospitals, doctors and therapists. He just wanted to get well! At least his last MRI had showed no sign of the remaining tumor but his head still hurt sometimes and he still hadn't fully regained his balance or strength. He'd also lost weight and his hair had not grown back as yet, so he was wearing a cap which made him feel unlike himself. He had never imagined getting back to normal would take this long or be this hard. His father's death had set him back more than he cared to admit but he was determined to put all that behind him and get on with life.

Daniel looked around the large room and saw patients on all kinds of equipment. Some were exercising their arms and legs using weight machines, some were struggling to walk using parallel bars to hold them up and the more advanced ones were on treadmills.

He felt conspicuous and self conscious. He was used to people staring at him but, in the past, that had usually been in admiration, which he acknowledged without conceit. Now he felt that they were wondering why he had this stupid cap on his head and why he looked so sick. He just wanted to get out of here as fast as possible.

"Miss Taylor," said the orderly. A woman in a long white coat and black jeans turned around. Daniel's eyes drank her in like a man deprived of water for a long time. This was the first spark of life he felt since his surgery. Her skin, the color of café-au-lait was flawless, her hazel eyes were beautiful and even with her long, light brown hair pulled back in a simple pony tail and very little make up on, she was gorgeous. She reminded him of Vanessa Williams when she became the first Black Miss America in the '80's. He felt a stirring in his body for the first time in weeks and almost smiled in relief to know that some things were still working.

"This is Daniel Tennant," continued the orderly.

"Thanks Pete," she said with a smile, walking over to them.

"Hi, I'm Kathryn Taylor," she introduced herself, extending her hand, "but most people call me KT. I'll be your physiotherapist." She didn't even seem to notice the cap, but then again he supposed she was used to things like that in her line of work.

Her handshake was surprisingly firm considering how soft her hand felt in Daniel's. He wanted to keep holding it. He quickly checked her left hand for a ring and was happy to see none.

Kathryn Tennant sounds even better and you wouldn't even have to change your initials, thought Daniel. Where did that come from? He closed his eyes and tried to clear his head. The drugs must be affecting my thinking!

"Hi, KT," he said sounding surprisingly normal in spite of the thoughts going around in his head. "Isn't it too soon to be starting therapy? My head still hurts like the very devil and I feel dizzy and weak."

"I'm afraid you're going to feel like that for a little while, Mr. Tennant, so the sooner we get started the better."

"Please call me Daniel," he interjected.

"Daniel then. We'll take it easy today. I'll just let you do a few exercises to assess your strength and find out which areas need the most work. You'll probably feel tired very quickly but that's normal. Don't try to overdo it; we've got about two months to get you back to your old self."

Daniel suddenly didn't mind if it took him two years to get back to his old self if it meant seeing her every week. He began to wonder if they took out something else from his brain apart from the tumor. What was he thinking? He didn't normally see the same woman for two months, far less two years!

Half an hour later Daniel felt that he never wanted to see Miss Kathryn Taylor again in his life! His head throbbed, his arms and legs felt weak and wobbly and sweat poured off his body.

"I wouldn't mind feeling this sweaty and weak if it was after a couple of hours of passion, but this is ridiculous!" Daniel joked trying to cover up how worried he was. Would he ever feel well again?

KT didn't crack a smile at his attempted humor. Instead she said: "Please keep your offensive comments to yourself, Mr. Tennant and let's focus on getting you on your feet."

Daniel frowned feeling somewhat chastened. Offensive comments? This was 2008 for heaven's sake not the Victorian era! Was she for real?

"My apologies," he said. "I didn't mean to offend you. That's just my way of trying to deal with how weak I feel. I'm wondering if I'll ever get back to normal."

Her face immediately softened in understanding and she squeezed his shoulder in sympathy. Her touch was strangely comforting to Daniel. In spite of his obvious weight loss, his shoulder felt strong and very masculine to her.

"Don't worry, you'll be fine. Recovery from brain surgery takes time so you need to be patient with yourself. Anyway, that's enough for today. I'll get one of the orderlies to take you back downstairs."

She offered him her shoulder to lean on to get back into his wheelchair.

"I don't want to make you sweaty," he protested. At least not in this way, he added in his mind. He was smart enough not to say that one out loud.

"That's okay, I'm used to it." But she wasn't used to the awareness she felt when he leaned on her. That was strange. She'd had many male patients but she'd never felt this immediate attraction to any of them. What was so different about this Daniel Tennant?

She was tall enough, probably about 5'7", to make leaning on her easy. He wasn't used to leaning on anyone, literally or figuratively, but it wasn't an uncomfortable or awkward feeling. On the contrary it felt good.

"See you next week," she said with a smile as she pushed his chair towards an orderly.

"Wouldn't miss it for the world, KT, even if it is torture," replied Daniel with a tired smile. Things were looking up for the first time since his surgery. No pun intended.

KT took Daniel's chart back to her desk to add her notes. She reviewed his information again and noted that he was 35, ten years older than she was and single.

And far too good looking she thought, even with the cap covering his head and the dark circles under his eyes. Where did he get off making crude comments to her? He probably saw nothing wrong with what he said. That may be his choice of lifestyle but it certainly wasn't hers. Still, he was very attractive and she admired his determination as he struggled to get through the exercises she'd given him, but he was definitely not her type.

"Hi KT," said Connie Haskins, one of the other therapists, coming up to her desk. "I see that you've been given the Merger Mogul. I'm devastated!" she exclaimed dramatically. "I wouldn't mind helping him get back on his feet. Or better yet, on his back," she added with a wicked laugh." KT ignored that.

"The Merger Mogul?" she asked looking up.

"You don't know who the Merger Mogul is? Don't you read the tabloids?"

"Uh, no!" replied KT emphatically.

"Well, your Daniel Tennant is known as the Merger Mogul in the business world. He does mergers and acquisitions and has a lot of money and a lot of women. Apparently he changes women with each season," she said with relish.

"He's not my Daniel Tennant" promised KT. "I could introduce you to him next time but if he has as many women as you say, then he's obviously not into serious relationships."

"KT not everyone is into serious relationships. Some people just want a temporary merger and if the rumors are true, his reputation as a merger specialist goes beyond his business dealings," Connie added wickedly.

KT held up her hand. "TMI!" she protested. "More information than I care to know."

"Just making sure you know who you're dealing with. I wouldn't want him to charm you into losing your head and becoming his next merger."

"There's no chance of that happening," declared KT. "Besides he's not my type and I'm sure I'm not his," she added.

"You're a beautiful woman so that makes you his type," said Connie walking back to her own desk.

'I'm definitely not interested in him,' KT told herself. So why did she feel a twinge of disappointment to hear that Daniel was a womanizer? 'That's for listening to gossip,' she told herself. Daniel Tennant was a patient and her job was to get him back on his feet, nothing more. And if she was looking forward to his next therapy session, it was only because she wanted him to get better quickly and off her roster.

misogynistic

12

~~female~~ innocent

Old stereotypes that ~~female~~ ~~must be pure~~ innocent

Daniel lay on Margaret's couch after a hot shower following his therapy session. He was waiting for the tablets he'd just taken to take effect and stop the throbbing in his head.

His thoughts drifted to Kathryn Taylor like a compass point to North. He just couldn't seem to help himself. Yes, she was beautiful, but so were all the women he dated. Maybe he was thinking about her because she was the first woman to interest him since his surgery. Whatever it was, he couldn't get her out of his mind.

He found her intriguing. A combination of professionalism mixed with a rare innocence that stirred something in him. If he was honest with himself, it was probably the predator's instinct to sample a new kind of prey. He should halt those thoughts. She was probably too young for him anyway. He figured that she was about twenty-three or four and definitely too innocent for him, which only made her more appealing. He honestly couldn't think of an innocent woman he'd ever known.

Vanilla. OK, his thoughts were not cooperating. He remembered the scent of her as she helped him back to his wheelchair. It was as if she bathed in it or rubbed her body with vanilla scented lotion. Just the thought of her rubbing her body with lotion was enough to make him stir restlessly on the couch. He would enjoy doing that for her. Not that it was ever likely to happen. Apart from the fact that he was her patient, she seemed kind of prudish so she probably didn't approve of casual relationships and those were the only kind he was into.

They were obviously chalk and cheese, oil and water, black and white, all the old clichés that indicated they were too different to mesh well, but he wasn't a merger specialist for nothing; he could find common ground. Maybe he'd invite her out on a date when he finished his therapy sessions. He'd never been out with someone like KT, in more ways than one. She'd probably turn him down. He smiled at the thought of the challenge and fell asleep with the smile on his face.

KT finished the Caesar salad with grilled chicken that she'd picked up from the deli on her way home. She had kept the garlic bread until last, as she tended to do with her favorite foods and now she savored the moist garlic-filled bread. Bread was her weakness. She took another sip of white wine and carried the trash to the garbage in her compact kitchen. She loved her apartment. It wasn't big but it was comfortable and homey. She'd really stretched herself to use what little creativity she had to decorate it by reading many décor magazines. It turned out very nice. At least her friends said so. Her Emma Shaplin CD filled the small room with soothing, modern opera music.

Her eyes scanned the sitting room and landed on the antique looking lady's writing desk in the corner between two windows. She had found it at a garage sale, during her décor phase, looking scarred and rejected and had taken pride in sanding it down and staining it until it looked almost like new. Her laptop was open on it but not turned on. That made a thought pop into her head: Google 'The Merger Mogul'.

"Thanks Connie," she muttered out loud. "This is entirely your fault."

'That would be like spying', her conscience protested. 'Not really, it's more like research,' argued another voice. 'Why do you want to know more about him if you're not interested in him?' queried her conscience. 'You should know who you're dealing with,' reasoned the other voice.

That makes sense, thought KT turning on the computer. She drained her glass and went to wash it while her computer booted up.

Sitting at her desk, she Googled 'The Merger Mogul'. Up popped the top three search results:

Merger Mogul – Is a free opt-in e-newsletter that provides expert commentary…

Mergers & Acquisitions – Sign up today and take advantage of member-only content…

Merger Mogul

*Commenting on the collapse of Shellbury Investments after its merger with Offshore Savings and Loans, The **Merger Mogul**, Daniel Tennant, CEO of Tennant Consulting said: "People don't...nytimes.com/ pages/business*

KT eagerly clicked on the link and read the New York Times article that had been published just a few months earlier. The Daniel Tennant quoted in that article seemed like a typical hard businessman. Not at all like the Daniel Tennant she had met today. 'Why am I researching him anyway?' she thought, but couldn't seem to resist Googling Images for *Daniel Tennant*. That gave her more information than she cared to know. There were quite a few Daniel Tennants out there but there he was, "her" Daniel Tennant in a business suit being interviewed by reporters, at a cocktail party, at a Knicks game, leaving a Broadway show. Apart from the business photos he was with a different woman each time. All of them were beautiful and glamorous.

Connie was right, he's definitely a womanizer. She suddenly felt depressed and as unattractive as she did when she was a teenager. She certainly wasn't in the same league as the women in Daniel Tennant's life. Why did I do that? she lamented. She quickly turned off her computer and went to the couch and picked up the book she'd been reading for several days but it didn't hold her attention. She kept seeing the images of Daniel in her head. That should teach you. Not only is he not your type, he's out of your reach so don't get any ideas KT!

*One week later*

Once again the orderly pushed Daniel into the Therapy department. KT was busy at her desk but looked up when she heard the doors open.

"Hi, Daniel. How are you today?" She greeted. She smiled briefly but it didn't reach her eyes.

"I'm much better now that I've seen you," Daniel replied. KT rolled her eyes but Daniel realized that he was serious even though he'd said it to flirt with her. She radiated a sense of peace that calmed the restlessness he was feeling, the impatience to get better quickly. "And how are *you*? You seem a bit serious today."

"I'm fine," she said, "And please save your flirting for someone who will appreciate it." She reminded herself of the images she'd seen of him on the Internet.

"Ouch! I promise to be on my best behavior," said Daniel even as he eyed her from head to toe, pausing for microseconds at interesting points along the way. She was dressed in jeans and a long white coat like the last time so he couldn't figure out why she looked so sexy to him. Maybe it was the enforced abstinence kicking in.

KT ignored him and said: "Let's get you started."

"You really love your job, don't you?" asked Daniel stalling.

"Yes, I love it and I want to keep it so let's get moving. I have rent to pay."

"I know it's more than that to you so you can drop the 'I just work here' façade."

"You're right," said KT relaxing a bit. "It's not just a job to me. I do love it. I love seeing the transformation of weak, barely functioning bodies into strong healthy ones when my patients reach inside themselves and find the strength and determination to overcome their challenges. It gives me a lot of pleasure to see the satisfaction on their faces when they accomplish even the smallest feat."

I'd like to give *you* a lot of pleasure and see satisfaction on *your* face, thought Daniel. Best behavior, Tennant, he scolded himself.

"So it really upsets me when a patient is prevented from receiving all the treatments they need because they don't have enough insurance or they can't get equipment because their insurance doesn't cover it. Right now I have a teenage boy who was involved in an accident where his friend was driving under the influence. He needs an electric wheelchair now to get around and another six months of therapy if he's to recover fully, but his mom is single and barely making it as it is, so the little insurance she has doesn't cover it!"

"I'm sorry to hear that," Daniel commiserated. He knew all about needing medical treatment and not having adequate insurance coverage. That's what had contributed to his mother's death. Medicaid was a help but sometimes it was the waiting period for treatment that determined the patient's outcome. Maybe he could find out who KT's patient was, without her knowledge, and provide whatever finance he needed to get him back on his feet. It was the least he could do and he could certainly afford it. He wished someone would have done that for his mother.

"What about you? Do you love your job?" She asked changing the subject.

Daniel thought for a while. Did he love his job or did he love what it gave him?

"I don't honestly know anymore," he confessed.

"What do you mean?" asked KT.

"I'm a merger consultant so my job is to find the right companies for my clients to merge with or acquire at the best possible price. I used to love the challenge of finding the right partner for a client and bringing them together. To be brutally honest, I really didn't care if they stayed together as long as I got my money, but now I don't know. So many mergers are failing. It's kind of like a marriage. Everything starts out looking good but after a while cracks begin to show up and soon a collapse happens and it can be messy as marriage without a prenupt. There are just no guarantees."

"Caveat Emptor!" said KT quietly. It still bothered her how cold and hard he had sounded in that article. She didn't want to be attracted to a man like that.

Daniel didn't hear what she said but it looked like she said Caveat Emptor. He couldn't imagine how she would have known about that quote and for some reason he hoped she hadn't seen the article in the New York Times.

"I don't believe in prenuptial agreements and in any case they're for people who have lots of money," said KT louder. "They may deal with the financial issues but they can't take away the emotional damage that divorce causes."

"As I've said before 'People don't go into marriage expecting to get divorced, but divorce happens.' So it's best to protect your interests."

"I know that divorce sometimes happens, but I believe in marriage. I see it as a lifetime commitment not some business transaction where I have to protect my interests, few as they are, so when I get married there will be no prenup and divorce will not be an option." She picked up his notes, looked him straight in the eyes and said: "Caveat Emptor!"

Let the buyer beware. Daniel didn't even need to know Latin to recognize that he'd just been warned. KT was not into casual relationships. She was a marriage or nothing kind of girl.

"Come on Daniel, you're not focusing today!" scolded KT. "You did these weights easily last week. Try again!"

"Are you by any chance a descendant of the Marquis de Sade?" snapped Daniel. He was tired and yes he was distracted but it was because of her. All he could hear echoing in his ears were the words: "I believe in marriage. I believe in marriage." Well that was certainly clear enough! She may as well have said: You don't have a chance Daniel Tennant. Anyway did he really want a chance with Miss Prude? She seemed like too much effort.

"Are you suggesting that I'm sadistic?" asked KT in a mock offended tone. "I'll have you know that I'm a professional and I would never intentionally hurt a patient. You're just not focused at all. What's on your mind, Daniel? Thinking about all those dates you're missing out on?" Even as the words left her mouth she was mortified. She'd never spoken to a patient in that way and certainly not about their personal life.

"I'm sorry Daniel. I shouldn't have said that." She apologized.

"I want you to say what's on your mind," Daniel encouraged. "I want to know what you're thinking." He was surprised to realize that it was true; he wanted to get inside her mind, not just her pants. That was a first.

"You *don't* want to know what I'm thinking," mumbled KT under her breath. "What I'm thinking is that you can do at least five more of these leg lifts," she said louder.

"You're all business, aren't you?"

"That's what I'm here for."

"And what if I want more than what you're here for?" Whatever happened to 'She seems like too much effort?'

"That's not an option."

"Why not?"

"I don't know what you have in mind, but I don't get involved with patients beyond helping them to get better."

"What about when they're not patients anymore?"

"I've never had a situation like that so I don't know."

"At least I have a bit of hope then," smiled Daniel.

"Hope deferred makes the heart sick," quoted KT.

"Then don't make my heart sick," said Daniel.

"That's assuming you have a heart in the first place," retorted KT.

"Touché," said Daniel. "This round goes to the lovely Kathryn Taylor."

KT laughed. She had enjoyed their verbal sparring. So did Daniel. He felt more alive than he had in a long time. If he felt this good just sparring with her, what would it be like making love with her? What was wrong with him? He had a one-track mind when it came to KT or maybe it had been too long since Angela.

"And no, I'm not thinking about the dates I'm missing out on," he said with a satisfied smile, resuming his exercises.

She'd hoped he hadn't heard that! That left ear compensation was beginning to kick in!

Daniel wanted to do something for KT. Just to please her. He couldn't remember the last time he had wanted to do something to please someone without an ulterior motive. He remembered how upset she was that she was unable to help the teenager who needed treatments that he couldn't afford. He could certainly help there.

He picked up his phone, scrolled through his contacts and selected the number for Luke Wellington. The connection was made after two rings.

"Luke Wellington's office, may I help you?" said the receptionist.

"This is Daniel Tennant. Is Mr. Wellington available?"

"You're in luck, Mr. Tennant, he just came back from surgery. Hold the line please."

The call was transferred and Luke Wellington came on the line.

"Hi Daniel, is everything OK?"

"Yes, I'm fine. I was just wondering if you could help me out with something." Daniel went on to explain the situation.

"I discovered that there's a teenager who needs therapy treatment and an electric wheelchair but can't afford either. I'd like to make an anonymous donation to the patient but I don't know his name or who to contact to arrange it."

"That's very generous of you Daniel. Call Mark Hubert. He's the head of Physiotherapy. He'll know who the patient is and he'll be able to arrange to get the chair and organize the therapy sessions."

"Thanks a lot," Daniel replied, ending the conversation.

Luke Wellington hung up the phone and looked thoughtful. He'd figured Daniel Tennant for a somewhat arrogant, self-centered type. He never would have imagined that he would care about another patient, far less pull his pocket to help them. Maybe his brush with death had changed him.

KT was restless. She'd been home for over an hour and she couldn't seem to settle at anything. Daniel Tennant was occupying her mind. She kept replaying their conversation in her head. 'And what if I want more than what you're here for?' he'd asked. Was he seriously interested in her or was he just flirting to pass the time until he was well enough to get back into his circle? What should she do? What she always did in a crisis. She went to the phone and dialed her friend and confidante Desiree Rodriguez. She'd known Des since high school and in fact it was Des who had invited her to the Youth Group meeting that had changed her life and given it new meaning.

"Hel-lo!" greeted Des in her upbeat voice. KT rarely heard Des sounding down.

"Hi Des, are you busy or can I pop by for a chat?"

"Sure, come on over KT. What's up?"

"I'll unload on you when I get there."

"Sounds serious," said Des.

KT made the short drive to Des' apartment, thankful to see a car pulling away from the curb and leaving a space for her to park. She knocked at the door and Des opened after just two knocks.

"Hi, darling," said Des and they hugged each other.

"Hi, Des."

Desiree was shorter than KT by about three inches but her effervescent personality made her hard to overlook. That and her black hair that was currently cut in a bob to her neck with the front bleached white blond. Her look and personality were perfectly suited to her job at an advertising agency. However, in spite of her punk look and her somewhat zany personality, Des was actually a great listener and had a lot of compassion.

"Shall we retire to the therapy room?" she asked leading the way to the kitchen. "I have some chocolate chip cookies and milk with our names on them."

"Sounds great!" said KT. She pulled out a chair and sank into it with a sigh.

"Des, I'm in trouble!" she burst out.

"Whatever it is can't be that bad and more importantly I'm sure it's not unforgiveable."

"Thanks for the vote of confidence Des. It's about one of my patients! His name is Daniel Tennant. He's recovering from brain surgery and has been assigned to me for therapy. Connie Haskins, one of the other therapists, said that they call him the Merger Mogul in the business world and she warned me to beware of him," shared KT.

"That sounds intriguing! Why is he called the Merger Mogul?"

"He's a merger consultant and the CEO of Tennant Consulting which apparently is very successful. I've also heard that he has a lot of women in his life but none seem to stay there for more than a few months."

"Oh, now I see. Did he hit on you?"

"Not really, although he has made suggestive comments."

"Well why don't you ask the hospital to transfer him to another therapist?"

"That's just it! I don't want him transferred. Des, this is the awful part, I've only just seen him twice but I'm very attracted to him. And he did come onto me a bit today and wanted to know if I ever get involved with my patients. He's probably just bored because he's still recuperating and not seeing anyone at the moment, as far as I know. I'm not even his type, if the photos on the Internet are anything to go by, and our lifestyles and values are poles apart so I don't even know why I can't get him out of my mind. Without sounding vain, lots of guys have come on to me but I've never been attracted to any of them like this before. What makes it worse is he's very cynical about marriage and has made it clear that he's just about making money."

"Let's Google 'The Merger Mogul' so that I can see what all the fuss is about for myself," said Des eagerly heading for her laptop in the sitting room.

"Don't you think this is like snooping?" asked KT guiltily.

"Well it sounds like you've already snooped my dear. But I don't see it as snooping, I prefer to call it research," said Des. KT smiled. That was Des for you. She felt much better after that confirmation.

A few minutes later Des whistled.

"So that is the Merger Mogul. I'm sure I've seen him before. He's hot KT!" she exclaimed as they looked at the images displayed for Daniel Tennant.

"I'm sure all the women in the pictures think so too!" KT commented drily.

"So now I understand your predicament. What do you want to do about this? More importantly what do you think God wants you to do? Maybe you've been brought into his life for a reason."

"Maybe. I hadn't thought about that," admitted KT.

"Well pray about it."

"Thanks Des. I'll do that. You're a woman of wisdom and a great friend as well. Pray for me too, especially that I'll be able to resist his charms!" said KT heading for the front door.

"You bet!" said Des giving her a hug.

13

Daniel tossed his cane into Claire's car and climbed in the passenger seat. He'd moved back to his house over the weekend since he was now feeling better, having finished with the radiotherapy three weeks ago. Today was to be his third physiotherapy session and he was looking forward to it. Actually he was really looking forward to seeing KT again.

"Hi, Claire. Thanks for coming to take me to therapy. I really didn't want Margaret to have to drive all the way to my place and, since you're not that far away, I hope you don't mind."

"No problem, Daniel. I'm glad to see that you're feeling better."

He supposed he should ask about the office but his interest was not really there. It was funny how a few months ago work was all he lived for and now it seemed so unimportant. Getting healthy again was his priority now.

"So how is the therapy going?" asked Claire as she negotiated the traffic.

"Therapy is a pain in the neck and everywhere else. I hate it but I can't wait to get there."

"What do you mean?"

"The exercises are hard and learning to get my balance back is very frustrating and I can't believe how weak I feel! But my therapist KT is great. She really encourages me. She's also very beautiful and very sweet. So that helps." He added with a smile. "She's a bit old fashioned though. One day I made a joke that I thought was fairly harmless about being sweaty after several hours of passion and she was not impressed." Daniel smiled at the memory. "Actually she told me off."

Claire raised an eyebrow, now very interested. "You said her name is Katy and she's sweet?" She had never heard Daniel talk so much about a woman. And she'd definitely never heard of a woman who told off Daniel.

"Her name is Kathryn Taylor but everyone calls her KT. And yes, she's sweet."

"Daniel they must have taken something else out of your head because I've never heard you refer to a woman as sweet before. In fact you probably don't *know* any sweet women. What's going on here, boss?"

"Nothing's going on Claire," denied Daniel. "It's a strictly professional relationship. Besides, she's not my type; she's too good and it would take too much effort to convert her. You know I'm into bad girls."

"Well maybe it's time you started to like good girls, Daniel Tennant," Claire suggested as they pulled into the hospital's car park.

"You don't need to come up with me Claire and I can get a cab back to my place after therapy," Daniel insisted.

"What and not meet the amazing Kathryn Taylor? No way, boss. I'll see you in."

Daniel shook his head. "That's what I was afraid of," he said. "Now be on your best behavior Claire."

Daniel pushed open the door to the Therapy department and KT turned around immediately as if she was eager to see him. Today her face lit up with a smile and Daniel's heart responded by picking up speed. The smile faltered when she saw Claire, immaculately made up and elegant in a black power suit, next to Daniel.

"Hi Daniel," she said as she walked towards him, her gaze shifting between him and Claire. "How are you today?" And how dare you get one of your women to bring you to therapy? she thought jealously.

"Much better now," insinuated Daniel.

"I thought an old pro like you would have a lot more lines," said KT drily. "You used that one last time."

Was the man serious? He was going to blatantly flirt with her in front of his current flavor of the month?

"Me, an old pro?" protested Daniel innocently. KT raised her eyebrows skeptically. Claire could feel the attraction between them and could see that they only had eyes for each other. She cleared her throat in a less than subtle hint and Daniel tore his eyes away from KT to glance her way.

"Oh, by the way, this is Claire Morgan, one of my senior consultants and today my driver. Claire, Kathryn Taylor."

"I'm pleased to meet you, Miss Taylor. Daniel's been singing your praises."

"Call me KT. Daniel's been singing my praises?" She threw Daniel a skeptical look. "I find that hard to believe. Last time he was here he accused me of being related to the Marquis de Sade."

"Really?" said Claire mischievously. "He told me that you were sweet."

"Sweet?" KT laughed. She felt a lot better now. This couldn't be one of Daniel's women if he told her that she was sweet.

"OK Claire, time to get to the office," suggested Daniel before Claire could say anything else. He wasn't sure if she was helping his cause or hindering it. What was his cause anyway?

"See you KT," she said.

"Bye," replied KT.

"You said I was sweet?" Claire heard KT ask as she closed the door behind her. She wished she could hear Daniel's reply but it was muffled by the closed door.

Claire pushed the button for the elevator. Wow! KT was not what she expected. Daniel's type was usually some glamorous blond or brunette, expertly made up and expensively dressed. KT was of mixed race, wore her hair in a pony tail with the minimum of make-up on and just a long white coat over jeans. She was not exactly glamorous in her work clothes but was certainly beautiful enough to catch Daniel's eye. Claire smiled to herself. She wondered if she could catch his heart as well. She hoped so. It was time that Daniel Tennant got himself into a permanent merger.

"OK Daniel. Today we're going to do some exercises to improve your balance. Are you ready for that?"

"Anything for you, darlin'," joked Daniel.

"Better not be too quick to say that," warned KT. "I might ask for something you can't give."

"I'd be happy to give you anything you want, KT" said Daniel. He realized that he meant it. He wanted to spoil her. Somehow KT was beginning to arouse something in him that went beyond the physical, although he wanted her in the worst possible way. He actually liked and respected her. He hadn't even made any suggestive jokes since that first day, although he did like to provoke her every once in a while with a little flirting.

"Anything?" replied KT reminding him of what he'd just said.

"Scout's honor," said Daniel, "Although I should warn you that I never was a boy scout."

"Why am I not surprised?" said KT drily.

"So what do you want?" pressed Daniel. "Diamond earrings, a necklace, a vacation in Hawaii…?"

"I don't want anything Daniel," smiled KT. "I have everything I need."

"You can't possibly have everything you need," protested Daniel.

"OK, probably not, but I'm content with what I have."

"Well you must be the first woman I've ever heard say that!" declared Daniel, still not believing her.

"What kind of women do you hang out with anyway?" asked KT half jokingly. She really didn't want him to answer that question.

"None like you."

"I wonder how I should take that," KT replied thoughtfully.

"In the best possible way, my love," suggested Daniel.

KT shook her head and rolled her eyes. Daniel was such a flirt. Could he change?

"Let's get to work," suggested KT.

"I think I need a wheelchair to get back down," said Daniel. His head was whirling from the balance exercises that KT made him do.

"No problem, I'll call one for you," offered KT. She went to her desk and made the call and then came back with a book in her hand.

"What are you doing now that you're back at home?" KT asked. "Do you read?"

"A bit when my head feels OK. Would you like to come over and read to me?" asked Daniel. "I have a penthouse apartment with a spectacular view of the city."

"No, I don't want to come over to your penthouse apartment and read to you," said KT lying through her teeth, "but I do have a book which I think you might find interesting."

He took it from her and read the title out loud. "Presence – An Exploration of Profound Change in People, Organizations and Society."

"Have you read it?" asked KT. Daniel shook his head.

"I read it a couple of years ago and I found it fascinating. It covers a broad scope of scenarios, not just business, but the underlying theme is that in each case something that they call "presence" somehow caused profound change to occur. There was a scenario where this Japanese photographer took photos of the crystals formed when water freezes and found that different crystals formed depending on the source of the water. He even did an experiment where he took photos of polluted water which was frozen and found that the samples had no crystal structure but after a priest prayed for the water he took another sample and found that the crystals were stunning! Isn't that amazing?" KT's eyes shone with amazement.

"So you think that prayer changed the water?" asked Daniel skeptically.

"As a matter of fact I do," said KT a bit defensively, "I think that prayer can change anything, even you," she challenged, "but I gave you the book because I thought it might give you some insight into the changes that need to happen when companies merge and maybe provide some solutions to help merged companies succeed," suggested KT. "I don't know, it may or may not help you, but I found it very interesting and very deep."

"Thank you, KT. I'm touched that you gave so much thought to the things I'm struggling with," said Daniel seriously. "Maybe we can discuss it after I've read it."

"I'd like that," said KT.

"That would be a first for me – discussing a book with a woman. I've had a lot of firsts with you," admitted Daniel. "I like it. And by the way, do you think I really need to change?" he added. "I thought I was perfect as I am."

"Yeah, right!" KT smiled even as she wondered if she could trust this Daniel or if he was simply playing her. Was she willing to risk finding out?

## 14

Daniel put down the book *Presence*, took up his cane and made his way into the kitchen to get a drink. His balance was improving daily and his head was feeling much better so he had been able to get through quite a lot of the book. In fact it kept him company over the Christmas holidays when he was not at Margaret's house although she had insisted that he come over and spend Christmas Eve and Christmas Day with her and Bob. It was profound and sometimes he had to read over parts to get what they were talking about but it excited him more than anything he'd read for a long time. He decided that he couldn't wait until he'd finished the whole book to discuss it with KT so he'd taken it with him to his last therapy session before the holidays so they could talk about it.

One of the authors had said in the book: "The only change that will make a difference is the transformation of the human heart." Daniel had argued that he didn't think the heart could be transformed. KT argued that it could and gave some examples of people she knew who had done horrible things in the past and then totally changed their lives when their hearts were transformed. Daniel said they were probably just pretending to be changed and deceiving people like her.

"Where do you know these kinds of people from anyway?" he had asked, protectively.

"Some of them are in the cell group I go to," she replied.

"What's a cell group? Is it some kind of group for people who used to be in jail and then get out and say they've changed?" he joked.

"Funny!" she said. "Actually I never thought about it like that but I guess the group is almost like that, except that the people *have* changed, not just claim to be, and they haven't been in jail the way you mean it."

"And why do *you* go to the cell group? What horrible things have you done that you're trying to get over? I can't imagine that there's anything really bad in your past, you're just too good."

KT smiled. "That's very sweet of you Daniel but none of us is really good. I believe that we're only good because God transforms our hearts."

"I don't believe that! They're lots of good people in the world and I'm sure that not all of them believe in God or even know that he exists. We are what we are."

"We'll have to agree to disagree," concluded KT. In spite of Daniel's cynicism, she now knew that he wasn't as hard as he had at first appeared. She had discovered, through Connie Haskins, who was a major source of information, that Daniel had bought an electric wheelchair for the patient she had told him about and was also paying for his therapy anonymously, or so he thought. She didn't know what made him do it, but the act of kindness opened a place for Daniel Tennant in her heart.

When Daniel was alone in his apartment that night, he thought about his conversation with KT again. Could hearts really be transformed and if so, could his? Did it need to be? He wasn't that bad, was he? Then he thought about the interview with the New York Times and the insinuations he'd made about Barton Phillips. Was that only a few months ago? It seemed like a life time. He remembered the way he had treated Angela the day his father came to see him and how he'd used Pamela even when he was seeing Angela. There were so many other things he had done that made him feel a bit squeamish now that he thought about them. All those thoughts made his head begin to hurt so he took some tablets and turned on a movie that numbed his brain.

Daniel poked his head around the doors to the Physiotherapy department, hoping to see KT. She was bent over her desk in deep concentration writing up some papers. Her pony tail was over one shoulder and her exposed nape looked so enticing that he was very tempted to sneak up behind her and kiss it. It took great control to just walk quietly behind her and trail his fingers down the back of her neck in a quick caress.

KT almost jumped out of her skin and immediately broke out in goose bumps. She swung around to see who the culprit was.

"Daniel Tennant," she exclaimed, "You scared me half to death! What are you doing here today? Your next session is in two days." Her hand clutched her chest as if she was trying to hold her heart in place. He looked devastatingly attractive now that his hair was growing back and he no longer wore the cap.

"I missed you, so I popped in to see if you wanted to go to lunch." He had missed her. Because of the Christmas holidays they'd had no session last week and he was amazed at how empty his week had felt without seeing her.

"Missed me?" said KT in disbelief. "You saw me just before Christmas. I can't believe you made Claire drive you all the way down here just to see if I wanted lunch? Wouldn't it have been easier to call?" Actually she had missed him too but she would never admit it. He had enough ammunition in his arsenal already. She hoped she could withstand his attack if it came.

"I took a cab. Anyway I don't even have your number," reasoned Daniel. "Perhaps you should give it to me now in case I need to reach you in an emergency."

119

"I can't imagine what emergency that would be," said KT but gave him her numbers while he added them straight to his Blackberry contacts.

"Great!"said Daniel, "So can you do lunch?"

"Well it so happens that my next patient is not due for another hour so I can do a quick lunch in the cafeteria."

"You're going to make me eat cafeteria food?" He groaned. "OK, but you have to let me take you to a real lunch, or better yet dinner, when I finish my therapy sessions with you," demanded Daniel.

"Only if you're on your best behavior," warned KT.

"Agreed!" said Daniel quickly. "And by the way, where do you get this impression that I don't behave well?"

"I've been warned about your reputation," admitted KT.

"My reputation?"

"Yes, your reputation as a womanizer. I've been told that you have a different woman for each season of the year! I'm not looking to be Miss Winter."

"KT, where do you get that stuff? Admittedly it may have been true in the past, but I haven't gone out with anyone in over three months."

"That's because you've been recovering from brain surgery!"

Daniel continued as if he hadn't heard her. "Come on, let's go and eat that unimaginative cafeteria food before your patient gets here," he said changing the subject.

After their plates were filled, Daniel found a table as far away from other people as he could manage and they sat down to eat.

KT said a quick silent prayer and picked up her bun.

"You're going to eat that bun?" asked Daniel incredulously. It looked very unappealing to him, especially smothered in melted butter.

"I love bread," confessed KT. "It's my weakness."

"I don't believe it, a weakness," said Daniel playfully. "Now I can win your heart by plying you with all kinds of gourmet bread."

KT laughed. "And what's your weakness?"

"My weakness is a certain physiotherapist who is determined to withstand my considerable charms," confessed Daniel half seriously.

"Funny," replied KT unbelievingly and Daniel let the subject drop. She obviously was not taking him seriously and he honestly didn't know at this stage, just how serious he was. What he did know was that he definitely wanted to get to know her intimately and he'd been around enough women to know that she was not immune to him either.

"How was your Christmas?" she asked.

"Lonely without you," he said truthfully. KT looked at him skeptically. "How was yours?"

"Great! I really enjoyed going home and being with my parents, my brother and his wife and my baby sister."

"I didn't know you had a brother and sister."

"Yes. My brother is about your age. He's an investment banker here in the city. My sister is in med school in Boston. She's 24."

"What else don't I know about you? Do you have a secret fiancée or anything like that?"

"No," admitted KT with a smile.

"Good!" Daniel smiled too.

"What about you?" asked KT.

"Do I have a secret fiancée or do I have any siblings?"

"Both."

"I'm alone in the world. I'm not seeing anyone and I'm an only child." KT was relieved at the first, if he was telling the truth and saddened at the second. She could feel the loneliness in his words although he said them matter-of-factly, and her heart softened towards him a bit more. "My mother died when I was in law school and my father died recently." Daniel felt a stab of sorrow.

"I'm so sorry. So how did you spend your Holidays?" she asked.

"My personal assistant, Margaret invited me to stay at her place. I spent a lot of time reading *Presence* when I wasn't over there. It's amazing! I've just read the part about the group from Guatemala, do you remember that?" She nodded.

"That was when a team of people from all different sectors came together to try to come up with a vision to rebuild the country after years of civil war."

"Yes. The Vision Guatemala team," Daniel continued, "and they were supposed to develop scenarios of how Guatemala could move forward in the next ten years. What I found really fascinating about the group was what happened when they started to share their stories of the war. After one person finished their story (the one about the bones of the unborn children of murdered pregnant women) they said that there was complete silence in the room and later one of them said that there was a "spirit in the room", another person referred to it as a "moment of communion". That episode made them really come together as a team because suddenly everyone knew why they were there and what they had to do."

"Then there was that old Mayan proverb or something that one of the authors mentioned. How did that go again?" asked KT.

"'We did not put our ideas together. We put our purposes together. And we agreed. Then we decided.'" quoted Daniel. "That's what keeps coming back to me. It's as if there's a key in there somewhere to unlock not just the problems in merged companies but in many other companies."

KT nodded, pleased that she had helped Daniel find his enthusiasm for work again in some small way.

"It seems that you're beginning to love your job again," she said.

"Or perhaps love what it can become," agreed Daniel.

After they finished eating, KT walked Daniel to the entrance of the hospital to wait for a cab to take him back home.

He took her hand in his and said: "New Year's Eve is in a couple of days. Will you go out to dinner with me? I don't think I'm up to a party just yet."

"I can't Daniel," said KT regretfully, "you're still my patient."

"So what?" he asked.

"So I live by certain principles and I won't change them just to please you." Although it was tempting.

"I'd like to please *you*," murmured Daniel in a low sexy voice. KT blushed and looked away.

"Then don't pressure me," said KT ignoring his innuendo.

"OK" conceded Daniel. "I can wait for two more weeks. I'm sure you're worth the wait."

KT wasn't sure if she liked the sound of that. Just what was Daniel expecting from this date? She hoped not more than she was willing to give.

## 15

Daniel walked into the Physiotherapy department with almost no trace of evidence that only seven weeks ago his balance had been impaired.  When he reached KT's desk he presented her with a beautiful deep purple orchid in an attractive ceramic pot.

"Beauty for a beauty," he declared.  The other patients and therapists in the room began to clap and whistle, making KT blush with embarrassment.

"This is beautiful, Daniel! Thank you! What's the occasion?" asked KT.

"I just wanted to add some color to your life as you've done to mine. And besides this is our last session, or have you forgotten?"

"How could I forget?" said KT.  She'd miss seeing Daniel every week.  It was amazing how quickly the time went especially since he'd only needed seven weeks of therapy to practically get back to normal. "I'm actually going to miss you, Daniel Tennant, although you're nothing but trouble."

"The only good thing about this is that since I won't be your patient any more you can go out with me now."

"Who says I want to go out with you, Mr. Tennant?" she asked coyly.

"I'm hoping that you do," said Daniel humbly, "And don't forget what you said about hope deferred."

KT smiled. "I wouldn't want to make your heart sick, now that I'm beginning to believe that you do have a heart," she teased.

"So how's next Friday?"

"I'll go out with you next Friday on one condition," said KT. "That you'll come to my cell group on Wednesday."

"Agreed! Is that the group with the ex-cons? That should be interesting. I can come and pick you up now that I'll be able to drive again."

"They're not ex-cons, Daniel. Don't you dare say anything like that when you come. Remind me to give you my address afterwards. Now let's get to work. Since this is our last session, I need to be convinced that you're really ready for the world again." Though she wanted him to be fully recovered she feared losing him to his old life again.

"Oh no, Mademoiselle de Sade is back!" joked Daniel. "I'm really going to miss this time together," he said seriously holding her gaze. KT's eyes misted up. She didn't know how she was going to survive not seeing Daniel walk through those doors every week. In spite of what she told Connie, she was afraid she was becoming very attached to Daniel Tennant.

"I'm going to have to find other things for us to do together because I can't imagine not seeing you every week," he continued.

"Maybe you can join my cell group. That way we'd see each other every week," she suggested half jokingly.

"I'll see," said Daniel. That wasn't quite what he had in mind.

*Wednesday night*

Daniel found KT's apartment easily. He called her from his car and waited while she came out, although he would have liked to have seen her apartment. He hoped she'd invite him in when he brought her back.

He got out of the car as KT locked her front door and walked down the short flight of stairs. She was wearing a pair of black jeans, a deep red sweater and a long black coat. Her hair was in its usual pony tail.

"Hi there!" he said holding open the passenger door.

"Hi Daniel. Nice ride!" approved KT eying the black Porsche.

"Thanks. I'm now getting used to the feel of it again after not having driven for so long. Want to drive?"

"No thanks, it's too powerful for me. I'm afraid I might hit it."

"I trust you, but maybe another time when we're out of the city." KT noted that he seemed to take it for granted that there would be other times. "You'll have to tell me how to get to your friends' house. What were their names again?"

"Richard and Ann Baxter. They're the cell group leaders. We usually have about 12 people give or take a couple. I told them that I was bringing a former patient of mine who had brain surgery but I didn't go into much detail."

"So what do you do at cell group?" asked Daniel.

"Lots of things: hang out, listen to music, sing, talk, pray, read the Bible, eat…."

"Read the Bible? Is it some kind of church?" asked Daniel, wondering what he'd got himself into.

"It's not *some* kind of church. We are the church."

Daniel had no idea what that meant. All he knew was this was not what he had in mind for a first date. Although technically this wasn't the first date, it was only the precursor to it. OK, he'd endure church if that's what it took to get a real date with her.

"Tonight we're just going to hang out and watch a movie."

With KT directing him, in about half an hour they pulled up to a sizeable house in a nice neighborhood. He got out and opened her door.

"Thanks," said KT feeling a bit nervous. She wasn't sure how Daniel was going to fit in at cell group. She hoped he'd be comfortable with her friends.

KT rang the bell and the door was quickly opened by Ann who greeted both of them with a hug and ushered them inside.

"Ann, this is my friend, Daniel Tennant. Daniel, Ann Baxter and here comes her husband, Richard. Richard this is Daniel Tennant."

Daniel shook hands with Richard and said, "Hi nice to meet you."

"Likewise" replied Richard.

"KT tells me that you've recently had brain surgery. You seem fine though," said Ann.

"Yes, I'm almost back to normal although I find I still get tired quite easily. KT was great in helping me to get back on my feet; that's how we met."

"Well you must be special because KT has never brought one of her patients to cell group," said Richard.

"Uh, why don't we go and join the others," suggested KT quickly changing the subject. Richard was not known for his tact!

Daniel was introduced to a room full of people who welcomed him so warmly that he immediately felt at home. It was a mixed group in more ways than one: there were about seven men and eight women, of several races and ages. Most of them were in their late twenties and early thirties although Richard and Ann were probably the oldest at about 40. He knew that he would have trouble remembering half their names. They all appeared to enjoy each other's company and to genuinely like each other. He and KT were obviously the last to arrive because as soon as they joined the others, Ann turned off the CD that had been playing in the background.

"We're going to watch a movie tonight," announced Richard.

"What are we watching?" asked one of the guys.

"Matrix. You've probably seen it before. It came out several years ago but I recently ordered the DVD so I thought it we could watch it and talk about it," said Richard. "Have you seen it Daniel?"

"No. I've heard about the special effects in it but I've never seen it."

"It's a bit of a guy film so you'll probably like it. Lots of action."

Daniel smiled as Richard started the movie while Ann passed out bowls of popcorn and put other snacks on the table. The room was quiet for the next two hours except for the sounds of the movie.

"Now that was amazing!" said David, one of the younger guys. "The action scenes were awesome, especially where they were doing flips and running up the walls!"

*alive in a virtual world*

*cell group*

"Yes," agreed Richard, "but apart from the action, the film had some amazing parallels to our beliefs. For example, the way everyone in the Matrix believed they were actually alive when in fact they were living in a virtual world."

"How does that parallel your beliefs?" asked Daniel, interested in hearing the answer.

"We believe that although we're alive we may not always be truly living as God intended because we're mostly slaves in the same way that the people in the Matrix were slaves to the machines."

"So what do you believe we're slaves to?"

"All kinds of things – desire for wealth and power, fame, illicit sex, alcohol, you name it. We're often controlled by these desires and we can't help ourselves, that's what makes us slaves."

"That sounds kind of hopeless," remarked Daniel.

"It is hopeless when we try to do things our own way, but we believe that when we ask Jesus to help us do things his way, then he frees us from slavery and we can live as God intended us to, not controlled by anything. That's like Neo taking the red tablet and being released from the Matrix."

"Ah," said Daniel. Now he understood what KT had meant about people in her cell group being freed from a type of jail.

"They also kept referring to Neo as the One and they believed that he could save the world," added in Ann. "In a way he paralleled Jesus, who we believe to be the savior of the world. Neo even died and came back to life, as we believe Jesus did, and in the end he called and told everyone the truth and left it up to them to make their decision about whether they wanted to continue in the Matrix or be free. Then he shot up to heaven."

"Wow!" said one of the women. "I never even thought of all those things when I first saw the movie."

"Yeah, that was deep," said Peter, another one of the guys. "It's true though. You can just go through life thinking that you're living and free when you're not, because you're really just a slave to something and you don't even know it."

Daniel realized that finding out he had a brain tumor and that he could die had made him start examining his life. He'd always believed that he lived life to the fullest, but was he really living or was he nothing more than a slave to the desire for wealth?

"So Daniel, will we see you next week?" asked Ann.

"Uh, sure. It's certainly been interesting."

As he and KT walked to the car Daniel asked, "Would you like to go for a coffee? I don't want to go home yet. Unless you want to come with me," suggested Daniel with a teasing smile.

KT mix ∞ cauc + BLK

"I don't think so. Coffee sounds good though," agreed KT wanting to prolong her time with Daniel. This was the first time that they were together outside the hospital and she didn't want it to end. Granted, she had to go to work the next day while Daniel could sleep in but she figured the time she would spend with him was worth a couple of hours sleep.

Settling into a booth of a popular coffee shop with their cappuccinos, Daniel asked KT, "So tell me about your red tablet experience. What made you want to come out of your Matrix?"

"It's a long story but suffice it to say that my initial high school years were not easy. Because I'm of mixed race, my mum is Caucasian and my dad is African American, I felt that I wasn't really accepted by either race. I was too black for the white kids and too white for the black kids. I was all messed up. I felt unattractive, rejected and I was lonely and insecure.

"I started hanging out with the Latin kids. That's when I met my friend Desiree Rodriguez. She invited me to a Youth Group meeting at her church where the youth pastor was talking about us being fearfully and wonderfully made and that God doesn't make mistakes and stuff like that and that we need to accept ourselves and each other for who we are because God does. I felt that he was speaking to me. So that night, when he asked if anyone wanted to be free from fears, doubts, insecurities and give them to Jesus, I did it. I felt as if a void that had been in my life was finally filled. I also discovered that I didn't have to prove myself to anyone or try to fit in. I could be just who God created me to be."

"That's great! So are you totally over your insecurities?"

"Sometimes they try to creep back on me but that's usually when I've gotten too far away from God and I forget all the things he's said about me. What about you?"

"I've never really had any exposure to God and that sort of stuff. I guess I believe he's out there somewhere, because I don't buy the Big Bang theory, but I've never given him much thought in the past. In fact I've probably thought more about him in the last few months than I have in all of my life before the tumor."

"Maybe that was the purpose of the brain tumor, to get your attention."

"That's what Margaret said to me the night in the hospital when I found out. Well, if nothing else, one good thing has come out of this brain tumor," he said taking her hand in his. "I met you." KT smiled and said nothing. She still wasn't sure what Daniel's agenda was.

"It's getting late and some of us have work tomorrow."

They drove back to KT's apartment in a companionable silence, with soft music playing in the background. Daniel seemed to be deep in thought, even as he pulled up to the curb.

"Thanks for the ride and the coffee. See you Friday," she said getting out.

"I'm looking forward to it," replied Daniel. More than you know, he added silently.

16

*Friday Night*

Daniel arrived at KT's apartment at exactly at 7.00 p.m. He rang the doorbell and glanced around the neighborhood while he waited for her to open the door. When he heard the door open he turned his head, saw KT in the doorway and immediately sucked in his breath.

"Wow!" he exclaimed. KT looked amazing. He had never seen her with her hair down but tonight her long, light brown hair was loose and fell well below her shoulders. She was immaculately made up and wore a pinkish red strapless dress that hugged her body from the scalloped top to where it ended just above her knees and cinched at the waist with a broad belt the same color as the dress. It was perfection; not too tight, quite modest in fact and yet very sexy.

"Wow!" he said again. She had certainly been worth the wait.

"Wow yourself. You cleaned up pretty well, Mr. Tennant," she teased taking in his well fitted black suit.

"Here, let me help you with your coat," Daniel offered. She held out a long, elegant black coat and turned around so that he could help her into it. Once she got her arms through the sleeves he adjusted the collar and lifted her hair from inside the coat. Having exposed her neck, he couldn't resist doing what he'd wanted to for a while. He leaned forward and ran his lips down the side of her neck.

KT shivered and spun around.

"You promised to be on your best behavior!" she accused in a husky voice.

"Believe me, I'm trying." Daniel's eyes belied his words as they dropped to her lips which were glistening with bright pink lip gloss, rather than lipstick.

"But you look stunning and very kissable!" murmured Daniel, his eyes darkening to black with desire.

KT almost gave in to the temptation to be kissed by Daniel. This was too much. "We'd better go," she said picking up a small handbag.

"If you insist."

"I do. So where are we going?" she asked locking the door.

"There's a new restaurant down town called The Black Pearl. I've never been there so I thought we could try it. It's supposed to be excellent."

"Sounds great! I'm looking forward to a meal that didn't come from a deli," she said as she settled into her seat.

"You don't cook?" asked Daniel.

"Not much," admitted KT. "I'm not that great at it although my Mum is a wonder in the kitchen. I guess I didn't get those genes. She, on the other hand, loves to cook and feed people so she'd probably love to feed a helpless bachelor like you."

"How do you know I'm helpless?"

"Daniel I can't picture you doing housework and cooking dinner. You strike me as someone who eats out five times a week and orders in the other two days. Am I right?"

"Close," laughed Daniel. "That's why I have to work so hard, so I can afford to eat out and pay my helper."

Daniel suddenly had a feeling of well-being. He reached over and took her hand in his. It felt so right he never wanted to let it go. What was he thinking? Never was a long time. He heard KT give a contented sigh next to him as if she was exactly where she wanted to be as well. He could get used to that sound. It made him feel wanted, not for what he had or who he was (he knew KT didn't care about those things) but for him, Daniel Tennant. It was an intoxicating feeling.

Daniel's car was driven away by the valet and he took KT's hand as they walked into the restaurant.

"Good evening, Mr. Tennant," greeted the hostess. "Your table is right this way."

"Thank you" replied Daniel.

"I thought you said you'd never been here," whispered KT as they followed the beautiful hostess.

"I haven't, I'm not sure how she knows who I am."

"You're famous," said KT, "or infamous. Will we have to dodge the paparazzi?" she teased.

"Hardly," said Daniel. He really hoped not. He'd heard that sometimes photos of him appeared in the tabloids for what reason he didn't know.

They were seated at a table that was discreetly located and given menus and the wine list. They both declined wine, Daniel because he was still on medication and KT because she wanted to keep a clear head around Daniel.

They perused the menu right away so that they could get that out of the way and made their choices. KT ordered a salmon crepe to start followed by wild mushroom risotto. Daniel chose oysters as his appetizer followed by a 10 oz sirloin steak.

"Salmon and risotto are actually my favorite foods but I haven't had a decent steak for ages," he confided in anticipation, "and I probably need the oysters."

KT laughed at him and said: "You don't believe that myth do you?"

"You never know and I may need all the help I can get."

"No you don't," replied KT emphatically.

"What does that mean?"

"That means I think you're already in overdrive!"

"It's just that I'm incredibly attracted to you."

"I bet you say that to all the girls."

Before Daniel could reply someone stopped at their table. KT looked up and saw a distinguished looking man who could be in his late 40s. Daniel groaned silently. Not tonight. It was Barton Phillips.

"Daniel Tennant. I thought that was you. I see you survived that brain tumor." The man actually sounded sorry that Daniel had survived.

"Yes, thank you for your concern, Barton," replied Daniel sarcastically.

"You always come out smelling like roses, Tennant, but I guess the devil looks after his own," said Barton with his parting shot.

Daniel turned back to KT, angry to see that Barton's words had upset her. "I'm sorry about that KT. That was just someone with a grudge. Don't let it spoil our evening."

"Was that Barton Phillips?"

Daniel's eyes showed surprise. "You know him?"

"No, but I read about him in an article in the New York Times when they interviewed you a few months ago about a merger that had failed. This is where I have to confess that I once Googled 'The Merger Mogul'."

Daniel laughed. "Confession is good for the soul, I hear. I'm flattered that you were interested enough to Google me. How did you know that they call me The Merger Mogul?"

"One of the other therapists told me. She warned me about your reputation but I guess I didn't listen."

"I'm glad you didn't. My reputation is exaggerated anyway."

"Really? That's not how it looked in those photos on the Internet and you seemed really hard and cold in that interview."

"I may have been that way before, but I've changed KT. I don't have the desire to run around anymore. I think I'm ready for a more meaningful relationship and as for business, I don't even like the name Merger Mogul and all that goes with it."

"I thought you didn't believe that people could change," she reminded him.

"I'm man enough to admit that I may have been wrong about that."

"Now that it suits your purposes," she replied. She really wanted to believe Daniel but had he really changed or was it because he'd been out of commission

*Barton Phillips = Nemesis*

for a while? Her thoughts were interrupted by the waitress bringing their first course.

The food was delicious and Daniel was particularly charming as he tried to change the mood that was threatening their evening. KT could see why women found him so attractive, he was a great listener and he made her feel special, as if he only had eyes for her. She could already feel herself falling for him in a big way. Not a good idea, KT she reminded herself. Their lifestyles and values were just too different.

Daniel gave his number to the valet and waited while his car was brought around. Suddenly a bright light went off in their faces blinding them temporarily and they only heard the sound of someone quickly walking off.

KT was a bit shaken when she realized what had happened. "I was just joking about the paparazzi earlier. Does that happen often?" she asked shakily.

"Not really. They probably don't have any good gossip this week and are scraping the bottom of the barrel. Don't worry about it."

The valet opened KT's door and Daniel got in the driver's seat. He adjusted the heat and asked, "Are you warm enough?"

143

"Yes, thanks," said KT.

"Oh, I just remembered that one of my colleagues is having a cocktail party next Friday evening. Would you come with me? To tell the truth I'm not really looking forward to socializing just yet, especially with the Wall Street players but I should show my face and let people know that I'm still alive."

"I really don't think I'll fit in with your crowd, Daniel and I'll probably feel out of place."

"I'd really like you to come with me KT," coaxed Daniel, taking her hand in his, while driving with the other.

"Jonathan and Cassandra are very nice and Claire and some of the others from my office will probably be there as well. You remember Claire? She dropped me to therapy a couple of times."

"Yes I remember her. She seemed quite nice and I liked her once I realized that she wasn't your flavor of the month," KT admitted.

"You thought that I was seeing Claire? And you were jealous?" Daniel laughed delightedly. "I would never have guessed."

"You needn't sound so pleased or I won't go with you to the party," threatened KT.

"OK. Not another word. Promise."

They reached her apartment in what seemed like a very short time.

"Are you going to invite me in for coffee?" Daniel asked.

"I don't think so, Daniel. Besides we just had coffee at the restaurant."

"You know that I don't really mean coffee, KT."

"I know you don't, Daniel, but I don't invite guys to my apartment at this time of night and definitely not if we're alone."

"What! Never?" asked Daniel. He couldn't believe what KT was suggesting. He'd always thought she was fairly innocent but not as in untouched.

"I don't share your kind of lifestyle Daniel. I don't sleep around. I never have."

"Are you saying that you're a virgin?" he asked incredulously.

"Yes," she admitted. "Is that so unbelievable?"

"Well you must be the last one in New York. How have you managed that? Guys must be coming on to you all the time."

"I've always been very protected, especially by my brother Paul so I didn't go on many dates in high school, at least not alone. At that Youth Meeting I told you about, I committed my life to following Jesus and doing things his way and that means waiting for marriage. So although I've been on dates, I only go out with guys who share my values and who understand that being alone can be a temptation so we tend to hang out with other couples. You're an exception. I've never been out with anyone like you before."

"I'm glad," said Daniel and in a way he was. He didn't want KT going out with anyone like him either. "So you're really a virgin," Daniel mused.

"Yes," confirmed KT, "and I intend to remain that way until my wedding night, as old fashioned as that may seem to you. I told you I believe in marriage and marriage is a covenant. Do you know how covenants were sealed in ancient times?"

"Yeah," replied Daniel. He was still trying to grapple with the idea that KT had absolutely no intention of sleeping with him, even if she was attracted to him. This was a first for him! He may be ready for a long-term relationship but he certainly had no plans to get married so where did that leave them?

He got out and walked around to her side of the car to help her out then walked her to the front door. She got her key out of her evening bag, unlocked the door and turned back to say, "Thank you for dinner. I had a great time tonight. The food was wonderful and the company wasn't bad either," she teased trying to dispel the tension.

"Thank *you*, KT. I enjoyed being with you." He stepped towards her and gently kissed her lips. He waited. KT didn't pull away so he tilted her chin up and deepened the kiss, holding her head in place as he explored her mouth with his. KT froze for a moment but then returned his kiss. Daniel's body immediately responded and he pulled her into his arms. They fit together perfectly like two halves of the same whole. KT's fingers locked behind his neck playing with the hair which had now grown to brush the collar of his shirt.

Daniel's hands caressed the contours of her back and moved down towards her hips, pulling her more firmly against him, while acquainting himself with her feminine curves. As he tasted the secret places of her mouth, he felt her body start to tremble against his and knew that he could take her to the point where her desire for fulfillment would overrule everything else. He couldn't remember wanting anyone more in his life. He felt for the door handle so that he could guide them inside her apartment.

*No, Daniel.* He froze! KT made a slight protest. What was that? Was it his conscience speaking?

What do you mean, no? he argued in his head, now a bit distracted. Nothing has ever felt so right!

*Feeling right doesn't make it right. It's not right in KT's heart, no matter how you're making her feel.*

That stopped him. Something stirred in his heart, a feeling of protectiveness for KT that was new to him, where he even wanted to protect her from himself. He pulled back with a silent groan, reluctantly opened the door and gently pushed her inside, trying not to focus on her confused face, and closed it before he changed his mind.    It was the hardest thing he'd ever done. He walked back to his car without saying a word.

"Are you satisfied now?" he asked once he was in the car, not even sure who he was talking to.

In spite of his physical discomfort, a sweet emotion erupted in Daniel's heart and he knew he'd done the right thing. He'd put KT's feelings above his own desires. Is this love? he wondered.

KT locked the door in a daze and leaned back against it.    One minute Daniel was here and the next he was gone.    She couldn't believe she'd let him take such liberties with her, touched her in places that no-one ever had, kissed her as no one ever did!    She was mortified when she recalled how she had kissed him back. What was worse was the fact that he was the one who stopped, not her. She felt so ashamed.

"Oh Lord, I'm so sorry.    I'm so ashamed! Forgive me.    Help me to do things your way and not to let you down or let myself down." Soon she felt at peace and knew that her prayer had been heard and that she was loved in spite of her weakness.    Then she headed to the bath to shower away the evidence of her date with Daniel. She wished it was as easy to erase from her mind.

17 *Praying after a Kiss*

The telephone rang just before 10 o'clock waking up KT.

"Hello?" she said in a gravelly voice.

"KT, what were you doing out with The Merger Mogul last night? Are you crazy? That man is the biggest womanizer alive."

"Paul is that you? What are you talking about?" mumbled KT to her brother.

"Let me read you this trash that my dear wife brought in from the supermarket bright and early this morning. There's a big picture of you and Daniel Tennant in the "Out on the town" section and it says:

*Merger Mogul Back on the Town*

*Daniel Tennant, aka The Merger Mogul, seems to have fully recovered from his near death experience following the discovery of his brain tumor last September. He was seen at Manhattan's newest and trendiest restaurant, The Black Pearl, last night with a sexy but mysterious Vanessa Williams lookalike…*

KT's eyes flew open. He now had her attention.

"I'm in the tabloids with Daniel? Oh, no," moaned KT. "Some photographer sneaked a photo of us last night but I didn't really think it would show up in a newspaper."

"Be thankful that Dad doesn't read this garbage. So what is the story?"

"There's no story," denied KT. "Daniel was a patient of mine and he invited me out for dinner now that his therapy is over. That's all."

"I hope so, KT because I don't trust Daniel Tennant as far as I can throw him and definitely not with my baby sister. Stay away from him! He'd swallow you whole and not even get indigestion."

"Oh, Paul, don't be so dramatic. Daniel's not like that anymore, he's changed."

"KT, people like Daniel Tennant don't change, they deceive you into thinking that they have and when you believe them they show their true colors."

That sounded familiar to KT. In fact it sounded exactly like what Daniel said when she was trying to convince him that people could change. He and Paul were two of a kind.

"Maybe I should give him a call," said Paul.

"Don't you dare, Paul Taylor! That would be so embarrassing! I'm 25 years old. I can take care of myself. I don't need my big brother protecting me anymore."

THE MERGER MOGUL

"OK. No need to get so hot! I'll back off, but I hope I don't hear anything about you and Daniel Tennant going out again. Stay away from him KT. I'm sure your innocence is appealing to a man like him. That is if he hasn't taken it already!"

"Paul! You know I'm not like that." KT was glad he couldn't see the guilt all over her face when she thought about how close he had come to the truth. "I know you love me but please stay out of my business. I can handle Daniel. Bye Paul." But could she? If last night was any example, she'd just better stay away from him.

Within minutes of hanging up the phone it rang again. It was Connie Haskins.

"Kathryn Taylor, you dark horse! Whatever happened to 'I'm not interested in Daniel Tennant, he's not my type and I'm not his'?" demanded Connie.

"Hi Connie. Have you been reading the tabloids too? No wonder those newspapers make so much money. It was just a date. There's nothing going on."

"I'm sure there's no such thing as 'just a date' with the Merger Mogul. Be careful, KT. You're so innocent I wouldn't want to see you get hurt. He's not over there is he?"

"Of course not! Thanks for your concern, Connie but I'll be fine. Bye."

KT pulled the pillow over her head and groaned. She really didn't want to get up and face the world. She definitely didn't want to talk to, far less see, Daniel

Tennant. She knew that he'd be nothing but trouble from the start.

Daniel wanted to call KT but he knew that she would probably be embarrassed and wouldn't want to speak to him. He'd had a rough night, thinking about her and the way she'd responded to him. She was a volcano waiting to erupt and he wanted to be the one to make her blow. He couldn't believe he'd walked away from that. What was wrong with him? He tried not to think about the voice that he had heard the night before. It couldn't have been God because he didn't believe that God talked to people, especially not to people like him. So maybe his conscience had been stirring. Not one to leave things unfinished, except for last night, he mocked himself, he picked up the phone and called KT.

KT was pouring a bowl of cereal when the phone rang. She froze. Instinctively she knew it was Daniel. She didn't know how but she just knew it was him. She let the answering machine pick up.

"Hi KT, it's Daniel. I know that you're probably at home and you just don't want to talk to me or even see me again but please give me a ring." He hung up.

KT put down the cereal box as feelings of deep shame came over her. She felt that she wanted to crawl into a hole and hide for the rest of her life. She groaned.

Why did she agree to go out with Daniel when she knew how attracted to him she was? He probably thought that she was a hypocrite. Just a few minutes before she was telling him that she didn't sleep around and next thing you know she was all over him like a hussy and worse yet, it was he who stopped. She groaned again.

The phone rang again and she let it go to the answering machine for the second time.

"KT if you don't pick up I'm driving over there. Would you prefer …?"

KT picked up the phone. "Hi Daniel," she said quietly, cringing all the while.

"Hi KT. I just wanted to apologize for coming on to you last night so strong especially after what you'd just told me. All I can say is that I lost my head. I'm sorry."

KT stood there in amazement. Daniel was apologizing for last night? It wasn't as if she'd tried to stop him, far from.

"Daniel, please don't say anymore, I'm mortified at my behavior and quite frankly I don't think we should see each other again, at least not alone."

"OK, if that's what will work for you, we can hang out with other people, but I don't want to stop seeing you KT. I'm beginning to really care about you. Why do you think I stopped last night? And believe me it was the hardest thing I ever did."

KT felt a thrill at Daniel's words. It was true, he did stop when he could have pushed her to forget everything but what he was making her feel, but he didn't. Could she really believe that Daniel seriously cared about her? She felt a surge of hope.

"Thanks Daniel. Maybe we could meet at cell group on Wednesday night if you want to."

"Great! I'll see you there. I hope you haven't forgotten the cocktail party on Friday. Will you still come with me?"

"OK," KT agreed reluctantly.

"I'll be on my best behavior," promised Daniel.

"Where have I heard that before?" asked KT wryly.

Daniel hung up with a satisfied smile. At least KT was speaking to him and he'd see her on Wednesday. He'd prove to KT that he could keep his hands off her if, in fact, he could.

KT hung up the phone and immediately called her friend Des. As soon as she picked up the phone KT said:

"Desiree Rodriguez, you obviously haven't been praying for me as you promised!"

"KT, what's happened?  I must admit that I haven't been praying as much as I ought to."

"Well that much is obvious.  I went out on a date with Daniel last night and almost ended up in bed with him!  My bed!  The only reason we probably didn't is because he stopped!"

"KT, you're kidding!"

"I kid you not," replied KT.

"You said that *he* stopped? That's amazing. Maybe my prayers did work," added Des smugly. "Seriously though, if he has that effect on you, you should avoid being alone with him."

"Tell me about it. Des, he actually said that he's beginning to care about me, that's why he stopped."

"Wow!  Maybe God is doing something."

"I hope so," confessed KT.  "I really hope so."

## 18

KT made sure that she arrived at cell group early on Wednesday so that she would get there before Daniel, if he actually showed up.  She was both looking forward to seeing him and dreading it.

Richard opened the door and greeted her with a hug. She handed him the chips she'd brought to contribute and headed to the living room where she began to help Ann arrange the furniture for the night.

"Hi KT, you're very early.  Isn't Daniel coming tonight?"

"I'm not sure.  If he is, he'll drive himself."

"I thought you two would come together."

"We decided that it would be best to have some space between us," said KT. "Things were beginning to get a bit intense."

"Oh," said Ann understanding. "By the way, where is Daniel spiritually?"

"I'd say pretty far from God.  He said that he believes that God is out there somewhere but he'd never given him much thought before his surgery."

"OK.  Well you know he's welcome any time. We'll just love him as he is and let God do the rest."

The members of the cell group began to arrive a few minutes later. Every time the door opened KT tensed, waiting to see if it would be Daniel. At about 8 o'clock everyone was there and still Daniel hadn't shown up. She didn't know if to be glad or disappointed.

"We'd better get started," said Ann as she put on a CD.

Just then the doorbell rang and Richard went to answer it.

"Welcome Daniel," KT heard him say in the hallway.

"Hi, Richard. Here's my contribution; some sushi rolls. Getting them made me a bit late. Sorry."

"No problem. We're going to be spoiled tonight!" exclaimed Richard. "Daniel's here," he announced leading Daniel into the living room, "and he brought sushi!"

KT didn't hear the cheers and enthusiastic greetings. Her heart had started racing and she tried all she could to avoid Daniel's eyes but she felt his compelling stare on her. Eventually she could withstand it no longer and she met his eyes.

"Hi KT," Daniel smiled gently at her.

"Hi Daniel," she replied, relieved that his face bore no indication that he remembered Friday night.

"OK everyone, let's get started," said Ann turning up the CD again.

Daniel went over and sat next to KT on the two-seater couch. She was acutely aware of him. He looked very attractive in black jeans and a black sweater and she could smell a hint of expensive cologne on him. His thigh brushed against hers and she withdrew a bit more to her side of the couch.

"How've you been?" he whispered to her taking her hand.

"Fine," said KT attempting to take her hand back.

Daniel resisted and kept her hand clasped in his, resting their joint hands on his thigh. KT had to admit that it felt right. Daniel squeezed her hand slightly and fought the urge to bring it to his lips. He tried to focus on what Ann was saying.

"Does anyone have anything they want to share, anything that happened this week?"

One of the guys, David said: "Yeah, I do. I just want to thank you guys for praying for me about that advertising campaign I was working on. As I told you I couldn't get a handle on the campaign and no ideas were coming to me. Well, on Saturday at about 2.30 in the morning, I suddenly woke up and ideas began to flow. It was as if a tap had been turned on. I couldn't even get them down on paper fast enough. I put together a basic Power Point presentation over the weekend and showed it to my boss on Monday and he loved it. Our clients came in and saw it today and they were blown away! It was exactly what they wanted. That was totally God!"

Everybody started to congratulate David and to say how awesome God was. Daniel looked around at them curiously. He glanced at KT beside him to see her reaction and found her examining his face as if to see what he was thinking. He raised his eyebrow slightly at her as if to say: That was God? She smiled and turned her attention back to the group where another guy was about to share his story.

"You guys know that I can't start my day without a Starbucks right? Well, I always go to the same one every day before I go to my office. Last Thursday I had this feeling to go to one a block further away so I went. Well when I was waiting for them to call my name I looked around and saw a guy I went to college with. I haven't seen him for a few years so we got to talking and exchanged business cards. It turns out that his family has a big construction company. He looked at my card and told me that this was a real coincidence because he was just about to tender the supply and installation of the air-conditioning system for a building they're going to be putting up soon."

"Jackson's business supplies and installs a/c systems," whispered KT into Daniel's good ear.

"So I asked him if he could send me the specs and the Bill of Quantities and give me the opportunity to price it. So he e-mailed everything to me that same day. I worked all day and night, priced it and sent it back to him the next day and what do you know, he called me yesterday to say that I got the contract. A major contract! Now that was a divine appointment. More important, I was able to tell him how amazing it was for us to meet in the first place. And now that we've made contact again, I can invite him to cell group sometime."

There was more celebrating and praising God although Daniel wasn't sure what God had to do with it.

"What's a divine appointment?" he whispered to KT during the celebration.

"It's when God sets up an appointment for you to meet someone for a specific purpose. In this case it was to give Jackson the opportunity to connect with his classmate again and to get that contract."

"OK," said Daniel skeptically. He believed that God was out there somewhere, but did he really get involved in people's business? Did he set up appointments for people to meet or give people business ideas? He'd never heard of God doing that kind of thing before but these people seemed to believe it, even KT.

Just then one of the women, whose name he remembered from the last time as Dana said: "I have a word for Daniel." Everyone went quiet. Richard immediately got out a digital recorder.

Daniel quickly glanced at KT. What did that mean? She squeezed his hand reassuringly.

"Daniel, the Lord is showing me that at a young age you felt deserted and forsaken. It's as if someone left you or rejected you (I don't know if it was one of your parents or both) and I hear the Lord saying: Though

160

father and mother forsake you, I will receive you."
Daniel tensed and unconsciously held KT's hand tighter.
How did this stranger know this?  He hadn't even told
KT about his past.

"Because of that you've protected your heart by not
allowing people to get too close to you and you've built
a wall around it and the Lord is saying: I've started to
take down that wall and I'm going to take away your
damaged heart and give you a new heart."

"And I see that when you were growing up you
lacked a lot of material things and because of that you
made a vow that you would never lack anything again
and you've kept that promise to yourself at great cost.
The Lord says you've excelled according to the world's
standards but now he wants you to excel in the things of
God.  He wants to use you to do great things for Him in
the business world.    I'm also hearing the word
'Oneness'.  I don't know if that means anything to you
now but in the days ahead the Lord will give you
revelation concerning that word. Thank you Lord."

Once again people began clapping and praising
God.    Daniel barely heard what they were saying
because he was in such shock.   He hardly knew what
happened for the rest of the night because he kept
replaying the words in his head over and over.  When the
group broke up for refreshments, he told KT that he had
to leave.  Richard took his e-mail address and promised
to send the word to him that he had recorded on the
digital recorder they kept for that purpose.

He hardly remembered saying his goodbyes or responding to the invitations to come again. KT said that she would leave as well and walked Daniel to his car.

"Will you sit with me for a while?" Daniel asked quietly.

At KT's nod, he opened the passenger door for her and then walked around to his side, got in and started the powerful engine, adjusting the heat so that the car quickly warmed up. He leaned on the steering wheel, looking blindly ahead and said: "Wow! That was the weirdest thing that ever happened to me! Is that woman psychic?"

"No," said KT softly, "she's prophetic."

"What's prophetic?"

"That means she has the gift of prophecy. Prophecy is when someone hears a message or gets a vision from God for someone else. What Dana said to you was a word of knowledge which means that God gave her supernatural knowledge about something that only you and he would know. God sometimes uses that to get someone's attention."

"Well he certainly got mine," said Daniel. "That was so accurate it was spooky." He shook his head as if to clear it.

"Does God speak to other people like that? Does he speak to you?"

"God is always speaking. Sometimes I hear him clearly and sometimes I'm not sure if it's him or my own thoughts."

Daniel was silent for a moment. Then he said, "Do you think God speaks to people like me who don't even acknowledge him?"

"I'm sure he does. Why do you ask?"

"When I was with you on Friday night I desperately wanted to make love with you KT," said Daniel looking her deeply in the eyes. KT looked away. "But when I was about to open the door to your apartment so that we could go inside, I heard a voice say: 'No Daniel'. I thought maybe it was my conscience or that I had imagined it. Now I'm not so sure. Maybe it was God."

KT cringed at Daniel's mention of Friday night but she said "Maybe it was. I'm glad you listened."

"I need to go home and think about this some more," said Daniel distractedly. KT didn't press him to talk about it; she knew that he was overwhelmed. In fact she was a bit overwhelmed herself but at least she now understood Daniel Tennant a lot better than she did before.

As Daniel pulled away from the curb snow began to fall. The thought of staying in New York for the rest of the winter was not appealing.  There and then he decided to fly to Barbados and spend the last two months before he went back to work.  He had a condominium on the luxurious West Coast that he'd bought a few years ago and he'd only used it twice.  He'd get Margaret to call his agent tomorrow and tell her to get it ready for him. The idea was beginning to sound more and more appealing; two months on a beach in Barbados with nothing to do but relax and do some thinking.  The only drawback was that he'd miss KT like crazy.   He wondered if she would fly out for a visit.  Somehow he didn't think so.  Maybe the separation would be good for them. Anyway absence was supposed to make the heart grow fonder. He certainly hoped it would make KT's fonder.

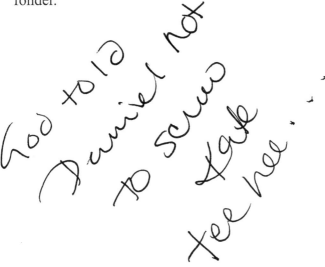

19

Daniel had spent a restless night. He kept replaying Dana's words in his head. Was God really speaking to him? How else would Dana know that his father had left and he'd felt rejected, that he'd made a vow that he'd never lack for anything again? That was amazing. And if it was God, why was he speaking to him now after all these years? What did he expect from him? What did he mean he wanted him to excel in the things of God? What were they and how could he excel in them if he didn't know what they were? What did oneness mean? The thoughts swirled around in his head until he felt dizzy. He must have fallen asleep at some point because when he woke up the clock was saying 6.54 a.m. but he didn't feel at all rested.

He made a cup of coffee while he waited impatiently for Margaret to get to the office. Once he got something in his head he was like a pit bull and refused to let go until he made it happen. The thought of getting out of Manhattan and spending some time just relaxing in Barbados had now fallen into that category and he was impatient to get it sorted out. To pass the time he started going through books that he wanted to read on the trip. *Presence* of course, Jack Welch's *Straight from the Gut* which he wanted to read again as well and *Built to Last* by Collins and Porras. He could always buy a novel or some magazines there.

At exactly 8.30 he called Margaret.

"Daniel Tennant's office," answered Margaret.

"Hi, Margaret."

"Daniel! I'd expected you to be back at work as soon as you got the OK to drive. When are you coming back?"

"Not for another couple of months, Marg. I find I don't have the urge to get back in the saddle just yet, which is why I'm calling you. I need you to call my agent in Barbados and ask her to get the condo ready for Sunday, then book me on a flight on AA to Barbados coming back just before April 1 which is when I'm due to come back to the office."

"One ticket? You're going to Barbados for two months alone?" Margaret asked incredulously.

"Yes Margaret, alone. I need to do some thinking."

"That's sounds wonderful Daniel. Make sure you get lots of rest as well. And try to keep out of trouble."

"I plan to Margaret. Let me know when you've got everything sorted out. I need to tell KT when I'm leaving."

"KT? She's your therapist isn't she? Haven't you finished your therapy?"

"Yes but we've been out once since then, Mother," teased Daniel, "and I went to her cell group a couple of times."

"Daniel Tennant, did you say you went to a cell group? And not once but twice? That's amazing!"

"Don't get carried away Margaret, I'm far from converted. Just do the bookings and e-mail me the itinerary."

"Right away, boss," said Margaret with a smile in her voice.

As soon as Daniel got confirmation of his flight and Margaret had spoken to his agent, he called KT on her cell. He hoped she wasn't with a patient because he knew she wouldn't answer the phone.

"Hello?" Luck was with him.

"Hi, KT, it's Daniel. I know you're at work so I'll be quick. I was wondering if you're free for dinner tonight. There's something I need to tell you."

"What is it Daniel? Can't you tell me now? Besides you know what happened the last time we had dinner."

"Dinner wasn't the problem it was afterwards. Look, I promise to pick you up, take you straight to the restaurant and back home. I won't even get out of the car. Scout's honor."

"Daniel Tennant, I know you were not a scout so don't try that on me. OK what time?"

"I'll come at eight and promise to have you in bed by eleven. Alone" he added with a smile in his voice.

"No kidding! Gotta go, my next patient just arrived," said KT.

"See you later," replied Daniel. "By the way this doesn't replace Friday. We're still on for that cocktail party."

"OK. See you later."

KT wondered what Daniel wanted to talk to her about. She knew it would drive her crazy until she found out. Was it about what happened at cell group last night? Was it about them? Not that there was any them. Maybe it was about their date. This was not helping. She used all of her will power to put it out of her mind and focus on her patient.

*Later that night*

KT hurried from her apartment and climbed into Daniel's car. True to his word he didn't even get out of the car.

"Hi Daniel," she said breathlessly.

"Hi KT. I hope you didn't have to rush."

"Not really. So where are we going tonight? Or is it a surprise?" she asked as he put the car in gear.

"I'm taking you to my favorite restaurant, The Bridge Café."

"Ooh, The Bridge. I've heard about that. I could get used to this," teased KT.

"I'd like you to," Daniel threw her a sideways glance. That's one of the things he liked about KT, she said what she thought and she didn't play games.

"So how's work?" he asked changing the subject. "Have you got any new handsome patients?" He really didn't have any claim on her and he realized that in the two months he was gone she could well meet someone else.

"The hospital has decided that my quota is one every six months and that was filled when they assigned you to me," she flirted.

"Kathryn Taylor, are you saying that you find me handsome?" he said smiling.

"There was never any question about that. But it's what's inside someone that's important, not what they look like on the outside."

"And is there something wrong with what's inside me?"

"I didn't say that, but if the cap fits…"

"I can never get a big ego with you around," complained Daniel.

169

"Maybe that's why God sent me into your life," she said half-jokingly. "So what is it you wanted to talk to me about?"

"Patience is a virtue."

"I'm afraid it's not one of my biggest, except with my patients," she admitted. "I'm more like 'God give me patience, but hurry'!"

Daniel laughed. KT was so refreshingly honest.

"Have you got any virtues?" she asked skeptically.

"Actually patience is one of mine. So you see I'm not beyond redemption. If I really want something I am prepared to wait until I get it." He threw a glance at KT to see how she took that.

"That's a wonderful trait," she complimented, not taking up the bait. "And I know you're not beyond redemption."

Daniel delivered his car to the valet and held open the door to The Bridge Café so that KT could precede him.

"Mr. Tennant, welcome back! Wonderful to see you again!" greeted the Maitre D'.

"Thank you Andre," said Daniel.

"I've put you at your usual table," said Andre signaling a waiter over.

"I'm impressed," whispered KT as they followed the waiter.

"That's the idea," Daniel replied smiling. "I had to pull a lot of strings to get a table at such short notice."

The waiter pulled out KT's chair and stepped back so that Daniel could seat her himself. He then offered them cocktails and left the menus and wine list.

"When was the last time you were here?" asked KT looking around in appreciation. Daniel was looking at KT in appreciation. While the view of down town Manhattan was just as spectacular as the last time he had been here it was the company that was even more compelling. Contrasted to the plunging neckline that Angela had worn that night, KT was wearing a classy black dress with a high neckline. Her hair was in a bun at the nape of her neck, but far from making her look severe, she looked very sophisticated and yet appealing with a few strands of hair curling around her face. Daniel knew it would take all his will power to resist trying to seduce her tonight.

"Earth to Daniel," she said when he didn't answer.

"Sorry. I think I was here a few weeks before my surgery, so it's been quite a while." He was glad she couldn't read his thoughts.

"I can see why it's your favorite restaurant. The view is amazing and I've heard that the food is fabulous. What do you recommend?"

"Everything I've had here is good but if you like seafood the salmon is excellent and so is the tuna."

"I'll go for the salmon."

"What will you have to start? And save some room for bread. They make great bread and I know how you love it."

"Yum," she said in anticipation, sounding like an eight year old.

They gave their orders to the waiter and as soon as he left Daniel said: "I won't keep you in suspense any longer. I just wanted to tell you that I've decided to go to Barbados for the next couple of months."

"Barbados? As in the Caribbean?"

"Yes. I have a condo on the beach on the West Coast of the island so I plan to spend some time just relaxing and thinking before I go back to work."

"That sounds wonderful," said KT hoping her voice didn't sound as hollow as she felt at the thought of not seeing Daniel for two months. "I'm green with envy!"

"You're welcome to come down for a visit," invited Daniel

"Uh, I don't think so, but thanks for the invitation," KT replied smiling.

"I meant that you could bring a friend. I've got two bedrooms. And I'll foot the bill."

"That's very generous of you Daniel. If I start to miss you really badly I might take you up on it," she teased.

"I'm serious! Don't dismiss the idea. I would love to show you Bar…"

"Daniel Tennant!" He was interrupted by someone stopping at their table. This was getting to be a habit! He looked up and his eyes connected to an ample bosom barely covered by a turquoise top. Angela! He hadn't seen her since the night at the hospital.

"Angela!"

"I called you several times when you were at Margaret but she wouldn't let me talk to you," she complained with a pout.

"I'm sorry about that Angel but I was feeling really low and didn't want to talk to anyone."

"You're forgiven, Mogul. It's good to see you back on your feet again. You look great!" KT observed the visitor to their table and noticed that she was practically eating Daniel up with her eyes. You didn't need any real discernment to realize that this was one of Daniel's women.

"Thanks. Excuse my manners. KT this is Angela Pierce, a friend of mine. In fact Angela probably saved my life by calling the ambulance for me and was with me when I was rushed to the hospital. Angela, Kathryn Taylor who was my physiotherapist after the surgery."

The ladies exchanged brief greetings.

"Well I hope to see you again soon, Daniel. We never did finish that weekend," she reminded him with a suggestive smile, before heading back to her table. Thank you Angela, thought Daniel. He braced himself for KT's response and she didn't disappoint him. She struck an exaggerated sultry pose and said:

"We never did finish that weekend," in the exact tone that Angela had used.

Daniel threw back his head and laughed, attracting the attention of several of the patrons, especially the ladies.

"Naughty!"

"I won't pursue that. So when do you leave?" she asked, deliberately changing the subject. She really did not want to know about the unfinished weekend. She could just imagine what it involved.

"On Sunday. That's why I wanted to see you alone tonight. I'm planning to spend some time thinking about the changes I want to make to my business. If Jack Welch could get his boundaryless revelation on Sandy Lane beach in Barbados, I'm hoping that I'll be fortunate enough to come up with something just as revolutionary to help merged companies succeed. I really need to find some new services urgently because merger consulting is taking a beating right now."

"So I've heard. I'll be praying for you."

"Thanks KT. That means a lot to me."

The dinner finished all too quickly for both of them and it seemed that in no time Daniel was pulling up to the curb outside of KT's apartment.

"Ten forty-five. You have fifteen minutes to get to bed. You see, I'm a man of my word."

"That you are, Mogul," teased KT.

"I'll pick you up at 6.30 tomorrow," Daniel reminded her. "Goodnight KT," he said, leaning over to give her a chaste kiss on the cheek.

"Goodnight, Daniel" she replied getting out of the car feeling a little disappointed. Daniel had behaved as promised. So why did she feel so let down? Was this the real Daniel Tennant or was he just lulling her into a false sense of security?

going to
Barbados

## 20

The elevator glided swiftly towards Jonathan and Cassandra Bailey's penthouse apartment. Jonathan had been to law school with Daniel and was now a partner in a prestigious law firm that handled a lot of the legal work for mergers. He and his wife Cassandra had no children yet and were well known for the great parties they often threw in their penthouse apartment.

KT had rushed out from work that day and bought a dress for the party. It was a black and olive and draped elegantly from her shoulders to overlap across her bosom, revealing just a hint of cleavage, hugging her curves and ending just above her knees. It had cost her a fortune but she felt that she might need a confidence booster. Her hair was pinned up in an elegant chignon with a few enticing strands teasing her cheeks. Daniel was enthralled by the alluring picture she made.

KT wondered at the wisdom of going out with Daniel alone again as she silently acknowledged how breathtakingly handsome he looked in his biscotti colored pants, teamed with a blue and white striped shirt and topped with a dark blue blazer. She nervously fingered the strand of faux pearls at her neck. She was really not looking forward to this party. The women there were probably beautiful, sophisticated and cliquish. KT wondered why Daniel even bothered to invite her. Daniel closed the distance between him and KT and took her hands in his, staying the nervous movements.

"Relax. You look beautiful." He pulled her closer and kissed the curve of her neck where it met her shoulder. "I've wanted to do that since I picked you up," he confessed. Before KT could respond, the doors opened into the lounge of the penthouse and someone said:

"Daniel Tennant! Welcome back to the living." It was Jonathan.

Daniel reluctantly turned around and putting his hand on KT's waist guided her from the elevator.

"Thanks Jonathan. It's good to be back. This is Kathryn Taylor. KT meet Jonathan Bailey." Jonathan leaned over and kissed her cheek, saying: "Welcome Kathryn. You must be Daniel's best kept secret and I can see why."

KT smiled, relaxing a bit. "Thank you Jonathan. Please call me KT."

"Well KT, what can I get you to drink?"

"I'll have a glass of white wine please."

"And I'll have a gin and tonic," added Daniel.

"No problem. I'll be right back. Cass is probably in the kitchen overseeing the caterers; I'll let her know that you're here."

KT looked around the room and was happy to see Claire Morgan engrossed in conversation with another woman at the far end of the living room. At least she knew one person here. The room was almost full of well dressed men and expensively dressed women, chatting and drinking and occasionally pausing to sample hors d'ouvres offered by passing waitresses. As Daniel led them further into the room, several people stopped talking to greet him, shaking his hand and welcoming him back. Curious eyes roamed over her as Daniel made introductions. Jonathan soon located them in the crowd and handed over their drinks. He was accompanied by a tall elegant blonde with warm brown eyes.

"Hi, Daniel. Great to see you looking so well," she said hugging him.

"Hi, Cassie. This is Kathryn Taylor, or KT as everyone calls her. KT this is Cassandra."

"Welcome KT," greeted Cassandra kissing her cheek. "Daniel's certainly kept you hidden. Have you known him long?" she asked, turning towards KT as the men started to catch up on business.

"Not really. I was his physiotherapist after his surgery."

"Oh, that explains it." KT wasn't sure what it explained. Maybe why Daniel was with someone like her rather than his usual glamorous type?

KT was surprised to realize how short a time she'd known Daniel.

"I just realized that I've only known him for a couple of months but it seems much longer. I guess he kind of grows on you." Cassie laughed as a striking blond, drinking champagne and wearing a cocktail dress that struggled unsuccessfully to keep her bosom well covered, joined the group.

"Daniel, it's wonderful to see you. You look great!" she exclaimed, throwing her arms around him in a hug. Daniel hugged her back, a bit too long in KT's opinion.

"Thanks Pam. It's good to see you too."

"KT, this is my friend and tennis partner, Pamela Highland." Cassie made the introductions. "Pam, this is KT. She's the one who got Daniel back on his feet. Literally. She was his physiotherapist."

"Well we're so grateful to you, KT. Does that mean Daniel can come out to play now?" she laughed.

KT didn't know how to respond to that so she smiled politely and said, "I guess that's up to him."

"I'm not up to playing just yet," Daniel said.

"Well call me when you are. I'd be happy to play with you," she added with a suggestive laugh. KT was sure she wasn't talking about tennis.

Trust Pamela. She wasn't known for her subtlety, especially after a few drinks. He'd better move on before she said anything more damaging.

"Well it was great to see you Pam. Excuse us folks but I see Claire waving at me."

"That was a bit abrupt," commented KT as he steered her away. "Afraid she would give away secrets?"

"There're none to give away'" assured Daniel. KT wasn't convinced. Pamela had seemed very well acquainted with Daniel.

"Hi guys" smiled Claire greeting them. "You look great KT and you too Daniel."

"Thanks Claire. You look wonderful yourself," replied KT.

"Thanks. How does it feel to be back in the real world Daniel?" Claire asked.

That confirmed KT's belief that the surgery had temporarily displaced Daniel but now he would return to his own world; the real world, as Claire called it.

"I'm not sure Claire. It's great to see Jonathan and Cassie and some of the others but I'm not sure that this is my scene anymore." That made KT feel a bit better.

"By the way, I'm flying to Barbados on Sunday for a couple of months. I'll be at my condo if you need me for any emergencies. Margaret will give Bryan the number or you can get me on my BB."

"I can't think of a better place to recuperate."

"I'll try to get some R&R but I also want to spend some time working on ideas for the business."

"I hope you come up with some good ones. We need them. And don't worry, we'll hold down the fort while you're away."

"Daniel Tennant! I don't see you for months and now I see you twice in two nights. What a coincidence!"

Daniel looked around to see Angela, tonight in a silky red dress that was a perfect complement for her dark hair which bounced around her shoulders. He hoped she wouldn't make any suggestive comments like she did last night. This was getting to be a bit much to deal with.

"Hi Angela. This town is obviously too small," he joked. "You remember KT? Do you know Claire Morgan? She's one of the Consultants at my firm."

"Yes to both. I believe I met Claire at the same party that I met you at. That seems so long ago. So you're definitely back on the town I see."

"Just temporarily. I'm actually about to fly out to Barbados for a couple of months to finish recuperating."

"Barbados! Lovely, but you look perfectly well to me," Angela said looking at him admiringly..

KT fumed silently while maintaining a polite smile on her face. The woman could not be seriously flirting with Daniel right under her eye. She obviously didn't see her as any competition and maybe she wasn't. After all, she wasn't willing to give Daniel what they so obviously were.

Daniel pulled KT to his side as if sensing her withdrawal.

"Thanks to KT. She did a great job with me." He bent his head and brought KT's hand to his lips for a kiss. KT practically squirmed with embarrassment as her eyes met Angela's over Daniel's bent head. Angela threw a brief smile at KT that didn't reach her eyes, as if to say: 'OK all yours, for now.'

"I'll bet she did," she said sweetly. "So when are you leaving?"

"Sunday."

"Well get some rest and try to stay out of trouble while you're there, although I know that trouble is your middle name."

"Hardly Angela and anyway I'll be on my best behavior," Daniel protested.

That's what I'm afraid of, thought KT, remembering the last time Daniel made that promise.

Daniel and KT left about an hour after that, for which KT was very grateful. She lost count of the number of women who came up to kiss Daniel and greet him, mostly ignoring her. She wondered how many of them he had slept with in the past. She probably didn't want to know. She was sorry that she had come to the party. It only confirmed what she already knew in her heart; that Daniel Tennant lived in a very different world to hers and she certainly didn't fit into it, nor did she want to.

They drove back to her apartment in silence. Daniel seemed pre-occupied and she didn't feel like making light-hearted conversation, especially when her heart felt so heavy. Daniel was sorry he'd asked KT to go to the party. He could tell that she didn't enjoy it and to tell the truth, neither did he. He was glad to see some of his old acquaintances but it didn't help that there were a few women there that he'd slept with in the past. He was glad that KT didn't know that, although he figured that she suspected as much. They weren't exactly subtle. He felt bad about it. Was that his conscience pricking him? Compared to them, KT was pure and untouched and he felt that he'd somehow dirtied her by exposing her to his previous lifestyle.

KT was reflecting on the evening and the women she'd observed. Some of them seemed as if they were just recycled among the men, Daniel included, moving from partner to partner. She couldn't fathom that kind of life. She had bought Daniel a gift to take with him when she slipped out to buy the new dress earlier in the day. Now she was in two minds whether to give it to him. It seemed kind of ridiculous after witnessing him in his element at the party. Would he reject it? Would he laugh at her gesture? The Porsche pulled up to the curb and parked behind KT's compact car.

"I'm sorry you didn't have a good time," Daniel said, turning to her. "But thanks for going with me. If it's any comfort, I didn't really enjoy it either. I think I've changed and I don't seem to enjoy that kind of thing anymore, but it's part of doing business and networking."

"It wasn't that bad," KT assured Daniel. "At least Claire and Cassandra were nice and most of the men were too."

"Yes, I noticed. They were practically devouring you with their eyes; single and married!" KT smiled. She hoped that Daniel was a tiny bit jealous, considering the number of women who seemed to know him intimately or would like to. She decided that she would give him the gift after all. He could certainly use it.

"Could you wait here for just a minute? I have something I'd like you to take on your trip."

She ran into the apartment and came back in a couple of minutes with a book in her hand. She slid into the passenger seat again.

"Another book? Is it as good as *Presence*?" asked Daniel.

"It's better. It's a Bible."

"Oh," said Daniel a bit skeptically.

"You don't have to read the whole thing cover to cover. Start with John."

"OK, John it is. If I promise to read it can I get a goodbye kiss?"

"That's bribery," protested KT but she leaned over and kissed Daniel on the lips. He caught her before she could move away and kissed her as if he was storing up the memory for the next two months. They were both breathing heavily when he stopped.

"I know I promised to be good, but that has to last for two months," he managed to tease huskily.

"You were good," she flirted getting out of the car. "Enjoy Barbados!"

"How can I when you're not going to be there?"

"I'm sure that won't be any hardship for you Daniel," she retorted drily. "You'll probably find lots of women there willing to make your holiday dreams come true."

"That's not going to happen, KT. Now don't *you* go meeting any other guys when I'm away," he joked, although he was quite serious. KT was becoming important to him and he didn't want anyone else to have her.

21

Daniel lay on his lounge chair on the beach with a feeling of supreme contentment. The waves were barely making a sound as they lapped against the coral sand. It was one of those truly beautiful days in Barbados with the sun shining brightly, a few white clouds randomly populating the azure sky and enough of a breeze for it not to be too hot. His Jack Welch book was next to the chair but he didn't really feel like reading at the moment, he was just enjoying the pleasure of doing nothing.

He'd arrived yesterday afternoon and after he'd been dropped off at his condo by a taxi, he just spent the rest of the day settling in and watching TV, something he'd done a lot more of while he was recuperating. He didn't even feel inclined to watch the business news as he used to in the past. He didn't know what was wrong with him but work didn't seem that important anymore. Maybe that's why he needed this time to refocus and find some solutions to the problems the business was facing.

The luxurious condominium was well stocked but he'd gone to his favorite restaurant, The Cliff, for dinner and had not been disappointed. As good as the finest restaurants in New York, it was nestled on a cliff overlooking the sea, hence the name.

His only real work was to figure out how to spend his days. Maybe he would rent a car and drive around the island or, better yet, hire a taxi to take him around because he really didn't feel up to negotiating the narrow roads. He'd been over to the east coast of the island just once and found it wild and untamed in contrast to the west coast. It was battered by the Atlantic Ocean and had waves big enough to attract both local and international surfers. He would love to show KT Barbados. It was a tiny island, just 166 square miles but with a rich heritage and had been a British colony up to 1966. He wondered what KT was doing now. Probably urging a patient to do some exercises that they didn't want to do. He smiled as he remembered telling her that she was related to de Sade, and the first day when she'd told him to keep his offensive comments to himself. He now understood her reaction. That was the lifestyle she had chosen and the values she lived by. It seemed as if it was going to be marriage or nothing with KT. Was he ready for marriage?

Not being one to remain idle for too long, he was just about to pick up his book when a feminine voice with a very English accent said: "Excuse me, but may I impose on you to put some sunscreen on my back?"

Daniel looked around and saw a very nubile brunette holding a skimpy bikini top over her generous bosom. It was unhooked at the back. He looked the other way to see if she was speaking to him or someone else, but no-one was close enough to them so he guessed she was talking to him. He groaned silently. This was not what he had in mind when he came out on the beach.

"No problem," he said graciously getting up and walking over to her lounge chair.

"I'm Mandy by the way. I hope this isn't a bother. I thought you were ignoring me because I called you twice before you answered."

"I'm Daniel. I wasn't ignoring you. I guess I didn't hear you because I recently lost the hearing in my right ear."

"Oh, I'm sorry," she said in sympathy a lot louder. "That must be really hard. I hope I'm not being too much of a bother but I really would like to get an even tan and not be red all over tomorrow."

"Thanks and it's no bother." 'Not unless rubbing sunscreen on a scantily clad female body is considered a bother,' he thought to himself. 'It's probably a very innocent request,' he assured himself as he squeezed cream onto Mandy's back. She wiggled a bit because of the coolness against her warm skin and practically purred when he rubbed it in.

"That's wonderful, Daniel. I'll have to find some way to repay you for this imposition," she said suggestively. Cancel the thought about this being innocent.

"That's okay," said Daniel finishing the job quickly. "I think I'll take a dip now, it's getting a bit hot out here." He jogged down to the beach with Mandy's

"Thanks" in his ear and dived into the crystal clear water. Whew, just what he needed to cool him down. He swam out until he couldn't stand up and floated for a while on his back. The last thing he needed was a Mandy distracting him. He was trying to change his lifestyle and the tempting English tourist was not helping. He hoped he could pack up his stuff and leave the beach without her noticing.

He swam and floated for about half an hour, long enough for her to fall asleep he hoped, and then made his way to the shore. He smoothed his hair back from his face and walked over to his lounger and dried off a bit with his towel. He packed up his sunglasses, slippers and book and made his way to the garden and up the stairs to his condo. Thank goodness that Mandy seemed to be dead to the world. Maybe he should have cautioned her about taking in too much sun but she was a big girl, he was sure she could look after herself.

KT wrote up the notes for her last patient and stood up stretching her back. She was tired as she hadn't slept that well the night before. Daniel was on her mind a lot. She missed him already and he'd only just left. How was she supposed to get through the next two months?

"You're looking rather tired," commented Connie from her desk across the room. "Late night with The Merger Mogul?"

"No Connie. Besides he's gone to Barbados for two months."

"Barbados? Alone?" KT nodded. "I'm sure he won't be for long. I really hope you haven't lost your heart to him KT because there's probably not a faithful bone in his body."

"There's nothing going on between us," insisted KT, "so it's not as if he has to be faithful to me." Still she really hoped that he wouldn't go back to his old ways, if he'd ever left them. She knew that being away would make it easy for him and she would never know. Wonderful! Why did she always listen to Connie? She must be a glutton for punishment.

"See you tomorrow Connie."

"See you KT."

She didn't look forward to going home to her empty apartment and pining for Daniel, so she decided to go shopping instead. A little retail therapy was just what she needed. She'd worry about the credit card bill when it came in. She wondered what Daniel was doing and who he was doing it with.

Daniel was sitting on his ocean front patio drinking in the amazing sunset with a gin and tonic for company. The sky was ablaze with pinks and oranges which were the back drop for the darkening clouds. He could hear the crickets beginning to chirp. It was amazing how after just a few days on the island you didn't notice them anymore. He'd gotten through quite a bit of his book today after he'd come in from the beach. He'd reached the part where twenty years earlier, Jack Welch was sitting on the beach at Sandy Lane, not too far from where he was now, when the word "boundaryless" popped into his head. The idea obsessed him for the next decade and he did everything he could to make GE boundaryless. Daniel wished that something would pop into his head to help him to solve some of the post-merger issues that his clients faced. Unfortunately the only thing that popped into his head was the fact that he'd like to share this sunset with KT. If she couldn't be there he could at least e-mail her some photos. That's when he realized that he didn't have her e-mail address.

He picked up his phone and sent her a text: Text me your e-mail address so that I can be in contact and send photos of this amazing island. Maybe you'll change your mind and come.

He hit the send button and waited for a few minutes, hoping that KT would respond right away. It would be an hour behind in New York, so about 5.30 p.m. KT would probably just be finishing work. He could always call her… He was interrupted by the sound of the

191

doorbell. Who on earth would be calling on him? He reluctantly got up and went to answer it. It was Mandy, wearing a sexy, short sundress.

"Hi Daniel, I hope you don't mind me calling on you but I just wanted to invite you to dinner as a "thank you" for doing my back today."

How on earth did she know which condo was his, he wondered? Oh yeah, he belatedly remembered the directory in the foyer downstairs.

"Uh, thank you Mandy but I've already made plans to go out for dinner," he excused.

"Oh that's too bad. How about tomorrow night then?"

Daniel really didn't want to go but how could he refuse again without seeming impolite? He drew on the health excuse. "I'm not really good company right now Mandy, I'm recuperating from an operation."

"But you look perfectly healthy to me."

"I'm on the mend but I still need to take things easy." He hoped she would take the hint.

"That's OK. You won't have to lift a finger to do anything. You just need to show up. I'll take good care of you." That's what I'm afraid of, thought Daniel.

"OK," he agreed reluctantly. "What time shall I come?"

"About seven. That will give me time to prepare everything."

"All right, see you tomorrow." He closed the door and went back to his gin and tonic which he now needed. Maybe Mandy was just being polite and friendly to a fellow tourist. He hoped so. He wondered what her story was and why she was staying alone in a very expensive condo far away from England.

Mandy made her way back to her condo, or actually her parents' condo. They were flying in the day after tomorrow after her dad finished tying up some business so she only had tonight and tomorrow before they came and spoiled her fun. Her dad owned several businesses in the UK and her mum was a typical rich businessman's wife, doing her charity work and appearing at all the social events that they were often invited to. She was tired of the scene and asked to come ahead of them to Barbados. She had finished her degree in English Literature three years ago and she hadn't quite decided what to do with her life yet. She was thinking of studying to be a chef because she really enjoyed cooking.

She was looking forward to trying out her culinary (and other) skills on Daniel. She had hoped he would come to dinner tonight but at least he'd agreed to come tomorrow. He seemed a bit reluctant but it couldn't be because he was married, at least she didn't see a ring.

Perhaps he was getting over a relationship or maybe it was just as he said, that he was recuperating. She wondered what sort of operation he'd had because he seemed quite fit. She smiled in anticipation; she hoped he was fit. She was sure she could get him to thaw out a bit. After all they were on a tropical island and there was something exciting about the anonymity of being far from home where you could be whoever you wanted to be and do whatever you wanted to do. After all that was what life was about, wasn't it?

## 22

Daniel made sure that he spent the whole day away from his condo because he didn't want to run into Mandy. He'd gone to Bathsheba on the east coast which was totally different from the west coast. The sand was a bit darker and coarser and felt wonderful to walk on. Powerful waves, stirred up by the high winds that were characteristic of that coast, battered the shore. It was truly a surfers' paradise and there were several of them taking advantage of the waves even on a week day. He spent a while sitting on the beach drinking a Banks beer and watching them dance their boards through the waves.

He enjoyed a real Barbadian meal at a small bar and restaurant overlooking the beach around two o'clock and then his taxi driver took him to an old restored plantation house which made its own rum in small quantities. He had a few samples of the aged rum both straight and in a couple of rum punches and was glad that he'd hired a taxi to take him around because it was certainly potent. The driver dropped him off at the condo around four thirty and he headed straight for his bed and crashed out. He certainly wasn't used to drinking that much yet since he'd been on the wagon for the last four months because of all the medication he was taking.

He woke up a couple of hours later, feeling less dizzy but he knew that the alcohol was still in his system. Maybe he should have a cup of coffee before he went over to Mandy's place. Lord knew he would need a clear head. He was sorry that he'd agreed to have dinner in her condo. It had "bad idea" written all over it. He headed to the kitchen and set up the coffee maker to brew while he went to shower and get ready for dinner.

He barely had time to drink a cup of the strong brew before he saw that it was almost seven. He grabbed a bottle of wine from the stocked cooler and headed out the door. Then he stopped, realizing that he didn't even know which condo Mandy was in or even what her surname was so that he could look it up downstairs. Then he saw her coming down the stairs which led to the penthouse suites.

"Hi Daniel. I just remembered that you probably didn't know which condo I was in so I came to get you."

"Good timing. I don't even know your surname so that I could look you up on the directory downstairs."

"It's Stafford. Amanda Stafford."

"Daniel Tennant."

"Wonderful, now that we've got all of that formal stuff out of the way let's get to dinner. I made a scrumptious meal for you. Did I tell you that I'm planning to go to chef school in September?"

"No, I can't say that you mentioned it but now I'm really looking forward to dinner."

"Good. I'm looking forward to it as well," she said. She led the way to one of the penthouse apartments which was lavishly furnished, if a bit English for his taste.

"So what are you doing in this big apartment all by yourself?" he asked.

"I'm not going to be alone for much longer. My parents are flying in tomorrow so I have to make the most of the time I have left before they get here."

"You make them sound very strict. Are they or are you underage?" he teased. "Just how old are you?"

"Oh I'm old enough to know better and young enough not to care," she teased. He wondered how old that was.

"I'm actually 24," she admitted. "I spent three years doing a degree in Literature and then I didn't know what to do with it so I've been bumming around for the last few years. But I love to cook so I think I'll have a try at chef school."

"That's great. I wish you success with that."

She led him to the dining room where the table was set with fine china, silver, linens and candles while soft music played in the background. It shouted intimacy and Daniel knew that he should probably leave right away.

"I'll bring everything out and perhaps you can open the wine you brought."

The last thing Daniel needed was more alcohol in his blood stream but he figured he would drink just one glass of wine with his dinner and then make his excuses as soon as possible and leave.

The dinner was delicious. Mandy was very creative in her cooking and blended some Barbadian produce with freshly caught Mahi Mahi which she'd grilled. He found himself drinking two glasses of the chilled Chardonnay which was a great accompaniment for the fish.

"I've made a tempting dessert," said Mandy.

"I'm afraid I'm too full to hold any dessert," admitted Daniel. The last thing he needed was anything tempting. "I ate way too much but that was wonderful Mandy. I'm sure you'll make a great chef."

She smiled in pleasure and said: "I'm glad I could repay you for rubbing cream on my back. I didn't burn a bit thanks to you."

"I'm glad I could help," replied Daniel getting up and checking his watch. "I really should go now but thanks so much for dinner. It was great."

"You're not going already!" whined Mandy. "It's still very early and I'll be ever so bored all alone." She glided over to Daniel and stood very close to him, their bodies just brushing. "Besides this is my last night without my parents and I wanted to have some fun," she pouted.

Daniel could feel his body responding to the obvious invitation. He knew that he had to leave now before it was too late. Mandy leaned closer and whispered: "I was hoping to show you how evenly I tanned." She put her arms around his neck and stood on tiptoe to reach his lips, catching the bottom one briefly between her teeth before soothing it. She pressed her body against his and initiated an intimate kiss. There was no mistaking her intentions. Daniel knew that she wasn't just being a friendly neighbor. He closed his eyes as he fought for control. He firmly unpeeled Mandy's hands from around his neck and put her away from him.

"Mandy, this is not a good idea," he tried to put her off. Far from being discouraged, she used the opportunity to quickly untie the halter neck of her sundress and let it drop to her waist. Daniel's mind barely registered that she was in fact evenly tanned all over, before she molded herself to him again and continued where she'd left off. This was definitely too much for any red blooded male to resist, especially one who'd been celibate for over four months.

Daniel shifted away from Mandy and lay on his back. He felt sick. It had nothing to do with the brain surgery or with the amount of alcohol he had consumed that day. He was sick with himself, sick about how he had given in to his body's cravings as if he was an animal acting solely on instinct rather than with self control. He also felt that he had betrayed KT although they hadn't made any promises to each other.

"I have to go," he mumbled to Mandy as he got up and dressed hurriedly.

"Already?" she asked sitting up and holding the sheet modestly over her, which Daniel thought was kind of ridiculous considering how they'd spent the last half hour.

"Yes," he said. "I'll let myself out." He got out of there as fast as he could.

He reached his own condo and headed straight to the shower shedding his clothes as he went, as if he couldn't wait to get them off. He came out minutes later feeling clean on the outside but the sickness inside him was still there. He knew it wasn't physical. He threw on a robe and went to sit on the patio hoping the sound of the sea would soothe the restlessness in him.

Oh, God! He thought silently. Why did I do that? He'd slept with many women and never felt this shame and regret. He knew it was because of KT. He loved her, yes he acknowledged it, and yet he had somehow tainted that love by sleeping with Mandy. He had let her down, let himself down and maybe even God and for what? A few minutes of pleasure. Another wave of guilt and shame rolled through him. How could he rid himself of this sick feeling?

*Start with John.* KT's words popped into his head. Would it help? He'd try anything. He went into his room and found the Bible that KT had given him in the pile of books next to his bed and settled back against the headboard. Flipping through the index he found John and began to read.

*In the beginning was the word, and the word was with God and the word was God.* That didn't make much sense to him but at least it kept him distracted and stopped him from thinking. He kept reading until he came to some verses that practically leaped off the page into his conscience.

*This is the verdict: Light has come into the world, but men loved darkness instead of light because their deeds were evil. Everyone who does evil hates the light and will not come into the light for fear that his deeds will be exposed.*

For the first time in his life he clearly saw something he'd done as evil and he definitely didn't want it exposed. He had slept with someone he had met just two days ago; someone he didn't even know or really care about and it was just for physical relief. He had taken something that KT considered sacred, that God considered sacred and desecrated it. He had used Mandy, just as he'd used many women before, even though she had literally thrown herself on him. He had a

201

choice, he could have left but he didn't. Shame ravaged him again.

"Help me," he whispered to God. "I don't want to live this way anymore. My way isn't working and I can't do this on my own. Help me to do things your way." When the words left his mouth, they took with them the enormous burden of guilt and shame, leaving him feeling clean and at peace. He didn't understand it and he knew he didn't deserve it, but he welcomed it. He began to feel incredibly sleepy. The last thing he remembered before he fell asleep was a voice saying: *I'm giving you a new heart.*

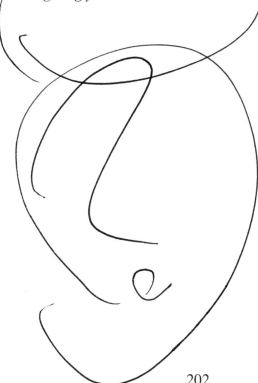

23

Daniel awoke with a feeling of well-being that he had never experienced before. He stretched and looked out of the open window of his bedroom and saw that it was another beautiful day in Barbados. Suddenly, everything came flooding back to him and he knew what he had to do as soon as possible. He had to find Mandy and apologize to her.

This felt like the first day of his life. It was as if he was Neo in The Matrix and had just taken the red pill and woken up in the real world. He smiled as he remembered that night when the cell group had discussed the film and how he didn't really understand what they were talking about. Now it was becoming clearer. Suddenly his stomach growled which made him get up, head to the bathroom to wash his face and then to the kitchen. He didn't feel like cooking anything so he ate a banana and then went to get ready for the day. He decided go to Sandy Lane for breakfast.

After a quick shower he hunted around for his Blackberry not sure where he left it. He wondered if KT had responded to his text. He found it on the counter in the kitchen where he'd put it down last night to get the wine. Sure enough there was a message from KT. He felt a pang of guilt as he opened it.

Hi Daniel, bet you're having a great time. My e-mail address is ktphysio@gmail.com. Looking forward to hearing from you. Miss you already. KT

Daniel cringed. The guilt he had felt last night returned in full force. He wrestled with himself whether or not he should tell KT about Mandy. His philosophy when it came to women had always been "never confess". But at the same time he didn't want any lies between him and KT. He didn't know what to do. He picked up the phone, his wallet and the keys for the condo and headed out to the beach. He would take a brisk walk down the beach to Sandy Lane. That should clear his head.

Daniel strolled lazily back up the beach after the sumptuous breakfast buffet. He was going to have to find a tennis club and arrange some matches while he was here considering the amount of food he was eating. Once his breakfast had settled, he would have a swim.

As he approached the condo he noticed Mandy lying on a lounger in the sun again. While he had used her as a willing source of relief yesterday, today he felt a compassion for her stir in him. She obviously didn't know her value if she would just throw herself at a man she barely knew. He walked over to her and crouched by her chair.

"Hi Mandy." She looked up from the book she was reading but didn't greet him. Daniel could tell that she was hurt by his abrupt departure the night before but she hid her eyes behind designer sunglasses.

"I just wanted to apologize for running out on you last night. I never should have stayed in the first place because I'm seeing someone at home." He detected a slight softening in her. "And, anyway, I'm sorry that I used you in that way. You're much too valuable to be treated like that by me or anyone else. I hope you know that."

He heard a slight sniff and saw a tear running down her face.

"No-one has ever said anything like that to me. Thank you Daniel."

"Friends?" he asked holding out a hand.

"Friends," she said with a slight smile, taking it.

"I'll treat you to dinner tonight and then I'll see you safely to your door. OK?"

"OK," said Mandy smiling.

Daniel got to his feet with a smile. That felt good.

Entering the quiet coolness of his condo Daniel felt a sudden desire to read more of John. Taking his Bible out to the patio he propped his feet up and began to read. If his business colleagues could see him now they would never believe it. He was soon engrossed in a story where Jesus was talking to a woman at a well. Jesus had told the woman to go and call her husband and come back. The woman replied that she had no husband. Jesus said to her: "You are right when you say you have no husband. The fact is you have had five husbands, and the man you have now is not your husband. What you have said is quite true."

Daniel had a sudden understanding that this was a word of knowledge, as KT had called it. Something that Jesus couldn't have known unless God revealed it to him. That was the same thing that had happened to him. He remembered that Richard had sent him an e-mail with the recording of the prophetic words he had received but he'd never listened to it. He went and turned on his lap top which he'd brought, waiting impatiently for it to boot up. Thank goodness there was wireless in the building. That's one of the things he liked about Barbados; it had all the modern conveniences he needed but was still quite quaint and not overly commercial.

He soon scrolled through his e-mails and found the message. He had to follow a link to listen to it online. He was still blown away at how accurate it was. He could even see that some of it was already beginning to happen. God was in fact giving him a new heart as he'd said. He now had compassion for a beautiful young lady who didn't know her worth. Maybe it was his new heart that stopped him that night with KT because in the past he would just have seduced her without a pang of conscience.

He wondered what God meant when he said that he wanted to use him to do great things for him in the business world. He certainly wanted to do great things and to help his clients. But how? And what did "oneness" mean? He was no closer to understanding that.

He wanted to talk to KT but she would be at work. The question came back to plague him again. Should he tell her or not? Would she forgive him? He desperately wished he could relive yesterday. He couldn't tell her over the phone, he'd wait until he saw her again.

He found his camera and went onto the patio to take some pictures of the view to e-mail to KT. He'd call her tonight when he was sure she'd be at home.

Daniel almost regretted asking Mandy to dinner only because he had to wait even longer to call KT. He made sure he had an early booking and dropped Mandy at her door at about 10.00 p.m. promising to meet her parents another time. As soon as he reached his own condo Daniel called KT. He could hardly wait to talk to her.

"Hello?" answered a male voice. Daniel didn't respond for a couple of seconds. His brain was trying to comprehend why some man would be answering KT's phone at this time of the night when she said that she never had guys in her apartment.

"Hello?" The person said again.

"Sorry, I must have the wrong number," apologized Daniel.

"This is Kathryn Taylor's apartment."

"What?" Daniel's blood pressure went up. Who was that man and what was he doing in KT's apartment?

"I'd like to speak to KT," Daniel demanded.

"May I say who's calling?"

"No you may not!" he said abruptly.

"Well I'm afraid you can't speak to her." Daniel was about to lose it when he heard an exclamation and scuffling on the other end and then KT said breathlessly, "Hello?"

"Who is that man in your apartment?" he demanded. He was surprised at the possessiveness in his voice and the jealously surging through him. As if he had any right to feel that way after his own behavior.

"Hello Daniel, I'm fine, thank you and how are you doing?"

"I'm serious KT. Who is that man?"

"Not that it's any of your business but that's my brother Paul. He and his wife are here for dinner. What gives you the right to question me anyway? Judging me by your own standards?" He winced. That was more accurate than she knew!

"I'm sorry KT, you're right. I had no right to question you like that. When I heard his voice I just lost it. I was being possessive when I really have no claims on you, but I'd like to."

"What do you mean by that?" KT held her breath waiting for his reply.

"Listen I can't have this conversation on the phone. Why don't you and a friend fly in next weekend? You can come Friday after work and fly out Sunday night. Or better yet see if you can get a couple of days of holiday and stay for a week."

KT was really tempted. She had a week of holiday due to her. She'd see if Des could go with her or else she'd ask one of her friends from cell group.

"I'll see Daniel."

"Is that a yes?"

"It's a maybe."

"Great! At least it's not a no. As soon as you know for sure call Margaret and get her to book the flights for you."

"I can't do that! She doesn't work for me, she works for you. And besides, what would she think?" protested KT.

"OK, I'll deal with Margaret. I can't wait to see you KT."

"It's not definite Daniel. I'll have to see if I can get the time off." He heard murmuring in the background and he could just imagine what her brother was saying. Daniel hoped that he wouldn't try to change KT's mind.

"I'll be praying that you can come," he said.

"Did you say praying?" asked KT in amazement.

"Yes, I said praying. I've even been reading John."

"That's wonderful Daniel," said KT quietly.

"I miss you KT," Daniel confessed.

"Ditto," she said and he smiled, knowing that her big brother was still within earshot.

"Drop me an e-mail as soon as you know something."

"I will. Bye Daniel." She caught herself about to say "Love you". She realized that she did love Daniel but she wasn't sure how serious he was about her. KT hung up the phone with a big smile on her face.

"What's that smile about?" demanded Paul.

"He misses me," said KT dreamily.

"Please KT, he probably says that to all the girls."

"Thanks Paul," she said drily. "He wants me to fly out to Barbados for a week."

"That's out of the question! Have you lost it KT?"

"Paul you can't tell me what to do. And no I haven't lost it. I'll take a friend if I go."

"I think Michaela and I better come with you and make sure you don't get into any trouble."

"You and Michaela would come to Barbados with me?" KT asked excitedly. "That would be wonderful. I'm sure Daniel would put you up. Although I think he only has two bedrooms. You guys could have one and I'll share Daniel's."

Paul was about to burst a blood vessel when he realized that KT was teasing him and started to smile.

"I'll see if I can arrange to be out of the office for a week and I'll let you know."

"I need to find out how soon I can take my week off as well." KT started to feel really excited at the thought of going to Barbados and seeing Daniel. She wondered what he meant when he said that he'd like to have claims on her.

24

Daniel waited impatiently outside the arrival lounge at Grantley Adams International Airport as the doors slid open and some tourists walked out. He still couldn't believe that KT was actually somewhere on the other side of those doors. When she'd called him last Friday to say that she could get a week off he was amazed at how excited he felt. He couldn't recall looking forward to anything so much in a long time. Even the thought of Paul coming didn't deter him. He was even prepared to give up his room and sleep on the couch so that Paul and his wife could have the guest room and KT could have his. He liked the idea of KT sleeping in his bed, even if he wasn't in it with her. He may be getting to know God for the first time in his life but that didn't mean he didn't still desire KT. It did mean though that he would try to do things God's way which meant not trying to sleep with her before they were married and he was now certain that he wanted to marry KT. He just wasn't sure if she'd feel the same way once he told her about Mandy but he had to tell her.

He saw the doors slide back again and this time KT walked through them looking around a bit uncertainly. She was absolutely stunning in jeans, short black boots and a black jacket with a long coat slung over her arm and pulling a flowered suitcase. Just behind her was a tall guy with her coloring and short curly hair who was obviously her brother Paul. His wife Michaela, a beautiful Latin woman, was next to him and reached only to his shoulder.

Daniel waved and KT caught sight of him. The smile that lit up her face made him even more certain of his decision. His heart started to race like a schoolboy's as he made his way towards her and held out his arms. KT walked into them as if she belonged there and in fact it felt like a homecoming for both of them. No words were necessary. Daniel hugged her tightly and buried his face in her hair. Vanilla. How he had missed that! He just kept holding her as strong emotions passed through him. He really didn't care what Paul thought at this moment. He felt that he never wanted to let KT go again.

He heard someone clearing their throat and reluctantly released KT from his arms but kept one of her hands.

"Hi KT," he finally said drinking her in with his eyes. His hug had already said everything he needed to say.

"Hi Daniel," KT said softly obviously moved by his greeting. "This is my brother Paul and his wife Michaela."

Daniel shook hands with Paul and gave Michaela a brief kiss on the cheek.

"Welcome to Barbados. I've hired an SUV now that you're here. Let me take you to the car park and then I'll go and pay the parking fee."

"Thanks for having us Daniel," Paul said. He would really have preferred to stay at a hotel rather than accepting Daniel's offer but he certainly didn't want KT staying at Daniel's apartment alone. She may be 25 years old but she was still his baby sister and he really didn't trust Daniel Tennant. KT believed he had changed, but Paul needed to see it to believe it for himself. He grudgingly admitted that he seemed genuinely pleased to see KT and hadn't even released her hand yet even as he took her suitcase and wheeled it to the Range Rover that he'd hired. It would be interesting to see what the week turned out to be.

Daniel opened the door to the condo and allowed the others to precede him. The drive from the airport had taken forty-five minutes on the ABC highway. Traffic in Barbados was getting to be just as bad as anywhere else in the world but, when he led them onto the patio, it was worth the trip. They looked over the wooden balcony and feasted their eyes on the aquamarine waves, stretching from the horizon to where they gently lapped against the white sand of the West Coast.

"This is wonderful," said KT excitedly. "I can't believe I'm here!" she added turning to Daniel.

"I can't believe it either but I'm glad you are," he agreed hugging her again.

"That is getting to be a habit," complained Paul half-jokingly.

"You'd better get used to it," returned Daniel pulling KT to his side. KT smiled up at him while Paul frowned and opened his mouth to say something.

"Be good, Paul," cautioned Michaela who was very much in KT's corner when it came to Daniel.

"Can I get you a drink now or would you like to see your rooms?"

"Drink first and then room," said KT "but you don't have to wait on us, just show me where everything is and I'll get the drinks."

Daniel was only too happy to do that as he led KT into the kitchen where he had her all to himself. Pushing her back against a counter he nuzzled below her ear, nibbled on the lobe and then dropped kisses all across her cheek to the corner of her lips. KT shivered slightly and turned her mouth towards Daniel's. That was all the encouragement he needed. So much for not touching her he thought. He couldn't stop doing that any more than he could stop breathing.

Daniel knew that he had to stop now and with great self-control he reluctantly released KT and kissed her forehead.

"I don't know how I'm going to keep my hands off you for the week," Daniel murmured against her hair.

"Don't worry, Paul is more than willing to help you," joked KT.

Daniel smiled ruefully and moved over to the cupboard to take down some glasses.

"Do you think the others would like to try some mango juice?"

"Sure, that sounds delicious."

Daniel fixed the drinks although he promised KT that it was the last time he would do so.

"I don't want you to think you have to serve us Daniel. We're imposing on you so we're hardly guests and I feel terrible that I'm putting you out of your room."

"KT, don't you know that giving you my room is nothing? Besides I like the thought of you sleeping in my bed," he added wickedly. KT punched him playfully on the arm and picked up two of the drinks to take back to the others.

"Would you guys like to go out for dinner or shall I order in Chinese or Indian?" Daniel asked when he joined them on the patio.

"Actually I'm feeling too tired to go out," said Michaela "so if you don't mind, I'll go with the take out. Indian please."

"No problem, I can order it from Sitar which is not too far from here and I can pick it up. They do the best Indian food in Barbados. Now shall I show you ladies to your rooms?"

Michaela and KT followed Daniel, complimenting him on the beautifully decorated condo with its coral stone finish and traditional mahogany Barbadian furniture. He showed Michaela to the guest room first and left her to unpack. Then he led KT to his room which was immaculately made up by the maid.

"Surely you didn't clean this up for me, Daniel?" teased KT.

"You know me well. A maid comes every day to clean the condo when I'm here which isn't very often."

He indicated the en-suite bathroom and told her that he would have to share it with her since the powder room had no shower.

"I feel terrible that you're sleeping on the couch Daniel and having to share your bathroom as well."

"It's no hardship and I'll enjoy sharing with you and having you in my bed. There's so much I want to show you and to talk to you about. You'll be happy to hear that I've read through John and I've just started Luke. I'm going backwards it seems." KT was thrilled to hear that and she wondered if Daniel was being impacted by what

217

he was reading. He seemed different somehow, more peaceful and less driven. Maybe it was just from being on holiday but she really hoped that it was God working on him.

"We'd better go back to the patio before Paul comes looking for us," suggested Daniel. He really didn't want to spend the whole week fighting Paul and, to tell the truth, he knew that based on his past, even up to a week ago, he wouldn't have trusted himself with KT either. That reminded him of Mandy. He cringed inwardly. He'd have to tell KT about that but not just yet. He just wanted to enjoy the week without KT hating him but he promised himself he would tell her before she went home. Hopefully she would understand.

Daniel spent the next few days playing tour guide for the others although there were some places he had never been to himself. They visited Harrison's Cave where the women "oohed" and "aahed" over the crystalline stalactites and stalagmites that populated the cave and the waterfalls that dropped into clear pools of water. It was amazing that all this existed under the ground. He took pictures of KT on the tram with her hard hat on as they drove through the cave. He took advantage of the few minutes that the tour guide turned off all the lights in the cave to demonstrate just how dark it was in its natural state. The lights coming back on made him reluctantly release KT's lips and they both laughed when they heard a girl behind them whisper rather loudly to her mother that the man and woman were kissing when the lights were off.

The next day they went on the catamaran Jammin' for a cruise and swam with the turtles in the warm Caribbean Sea when the boat anchored further along the West Coast from his condo. Daniel was happy that he'd booked the cruise when he saw how thrilled KT was by the turtles swimming unafraid all around them.

They took a walk around Bridgetown which boasted having the third oldest Parliament in the entire Commonwealth, having been established in 1639, and took pictures of the two bridges which gave the city its name. Afterwards they ate at a restaurant overlooking the Careenage where a number of private yachts were berthed.

The week was speeding by faster than Daniel would have liked. He was happy that they hadn't run into Mandy and then he remembered, with relief, that she had mentioned going to Mustique, a tiny island in the nearby Grenadines, with her parents to visit some friends for a week.

On Thursday, KT and Michaela left the men to go shopping in Holetown, a nearby town, for souvenirs. They said that they would take a bus so that they could experience the local culture. The men were more than happy to laze around the condo rather than go shopping.

Daniel and Paul sat on the patio sipping rum punches and enjoying the view. The silence was surprisingly companionable as both men weren't big talkers. Eventually Paul asked: "When are you coming back to Manhattan? Things are getting fairly serious. Businesses are cutting staff like crazy and foreclosures are skyrocketing. Aren't you worried about your business?"

"I've been watching the business news from here and yes I am getting concerned. Before this whole thing we were trying to come up with some new consulting services so that we wouldn't be relying so heavily on mergers and acquisitions. In fact, since my surgery, I've been feeling dissatisfied with the merger side of things in any case. Too many of them have been failing and in the past I can't really say I've cared much once my bill got paid, but now I find that it's not enough. So I'm looking for ways to help with the post-merger issues so that more mergers succeed. I'm going back to work in April but I'm afraid I'm no closer to a solution as yet."

"Well if Jack Welch could get a brainstorm here, you should be able to," encouraged Paul.

"That's what I'm hoping," Daniel agreed with a slight smile. They thought alike in many ways he'd discovered over the last few days and he was beginning to like Paul.

"So what are your intentions towards KT?" asked Paul suddenly but not unexpectedly. Daniel knew that it would be coming; he was surprised that Paul had restrained himself this long.

"They're completely honorable," replied Daniel. Paul looked skeptical.

"Look, I know my reputation in the past hasn't been the best, but I'm really trying to change and I'm serious about KT. In fact I'm thinking about marriage for the first time in my life."

"Well I'm glad to hear that. I had warned KT to stay away from you but seeing the two of you together this week, how happy you make her, I've changed my mind and I'd be glad to have you for a brother-in-law."

"Thanks Paul." He knew then and there that he had to tell Paul about Mandy and ask his opinion on how best to break it to KT. He'd probably lose his respect but nevertheless he drew in a breath and said: "I've done something pretty sick and when I tell KT, I'm not sure she'll even want to see me anymore, far less marry me." Daniel paused and then confessed: "I slept with someone a couple of days after I got here."

"What? You're talking three weeks ago?" Paul erupted. Daniel held up his hand.

"She literally threw herself at me and it had been a while, with this surgery and everything, and I didn't fight it. I feel sick about it and I know that I betrayed KT but it didn't mean anything which makes it even worse. I've even apologized to the girl but I don't know how to tell KT about it." He closed his eyes as a wave of regret coursed through him once again.

"Look, if I were you I wouldn't tell her anything." Daniel's eyes snapped open. That was the last thing he expected Paul to say. "At least, not while we're on holiday because you'll ruin the rest of her time here and then we'll go back home and for the next month or so she'll be wondering what you're doing and who you're doing it with. It will torment her."

Daniel saw the wisdom in that and agreed. "OK, I'll wait until I get back to talk to her."

"In the mean time, keep your zip up," warned Paul "and I would recommend an AIDS test!"

Daniel knew he deserved that and, given his past, he owed it to KT to make sure he was safe before he asked her to marry him.

"Thanks Paul." Paul nodded, clearly not comfortable with Daniel's confession but as a man himself he could understand how it could happen. For Daniel's sake he hoped that KT would as well.

## 25

Sleep was not easy in coming that night because the conversation with Paul kept playing in his mind. He'd decided to take Paul's advice and not say anything to KT but he felt that the longer he kept the truth from her, the worse it was going to be. He knew that he was probably more quiet than usual when KT and Michaela came back from shopping and he caught KT giving Paul some penetrating stares as if she felt he had done something to upset Daniel, which only made him feel worse.

At about 1.15 am he turned on the lamp and picked up the Bible which was on the end table and flicked through the New Testament and eventually landed on a verse that said: Come to me all who are weary and heavy laden and I will give you rest." Well, he certainly was heavy laden with guilt and he needed rest so he simply said: "Lord I need rest from this guilt. Please help me to find the right words to tell KT and help her to forgive me when I tell her the truth." Having said that, he realized that tormenting himself with his thoughts was not helping so he deliberately stilled his mind and eventually fell asleep.

In spite of his restless night Daniel woke up very early, before the sun had even come up fully. He could hardly believe it was Friday already and KT would be leaving the next day. Something had woken him up but he wasn't sure what it was. He lay there for a few minutes and eventually bits of a dream he had came back to him. He was on some sort of a construction site but he didn't recognize what the people were building and, even as he was trying to work it out in the dream, he heard the words: *Indeed the people are one and they all have one language and this is what they begin to do; now nothing that they propose to do will be withheld from them.*

What did the words mean? Where were they from? He wanted to wake up KT and ask her if she knew what they meant since they sounded like something from the Bible. Instead he went to the small powder room and washed his face and brushed his teeth and then quietly opened the French door so that he could sit on the patio and wait for the sun to come up. He loved this time of the day which was so fresh and unspoiled, like KT, he thought with a smile. His thoughts must have conjured her up because he heard the door open a couple of minutes later and looked around to see her in silky Mickey Mouse pajamas with her hair mussed up from sleeping. He liked the fact that she didn't bother to fix it before she came to find him. She looked gorgeous. Daniel held out his arms and she came and sat on his lap. This was the first time they'd really been alone for the week. He held her tight.

"Good morning sunshine," he whispered.

"Good morning to you too," she said burrowing into him. "Um, you're so warm and nice. I'm surprised at how chilly it is out here."

"That's because you've become acclimatized to the Barbadian weather. Tomorrow when you get back to New York, you'll think that this was warm."

"Don't remind me. I don't want to go back," groaned KT.

"I don't want you to either. This week was wonderful. This is the best time I've ever had in my life."

"Yeah, right." She believed that Daniel was just saying that for her benefit.

"No, I'm serious KT. I never had much to enjoy in life when I was young. My dad left home when I was ten and never looked back..." And Daniel shared his story for the first time in his life.

"I've never told anyone that before so I was really shocked by Dana's prophecy," he confided.

"I'm glad you told me, Daniel. It helps me to understand you so much better. Thank you." She kissed him softly on the lips.

"That is not a good idea KT, especially with you sitting on my lap." KT was about to jump up when he pulled her back against his chest and they just sat looking at the horizon as the new day began to dawn. Daniel would have loved to ask KT to marry him there and then, but he knew it wouldn't be fair to her. He had to tell her about Mandy first and hope that she would find it in her heart to forgive him, far less marry him.

Suddenly he remembered the words that he'd heard in his dream or when he woke up he wasn't sure which and asked: "KT have you ever heard the words: 'The people are one and they all have one language and this is what they begin to do; now nothing…"

"…they propose to do will be withheld from them," she finished.

"Yes," he said excitedly, "Where are they from?"

"From the story of the Tower of Babel in Genesis. Why?"

"I woke up with them in my head but I haven't read Genesis. That's weird."

"Maybe God is speaking to you."

"What's the story about?"asked Daniel.

"It's about a group of people who got together and agreed to build a city and a tower that reached up to heaven. They were succeeding too and the Bible says that God came down to see what they were doing and that's when he said "The people are one…"

"Oneness!" Daniel interrupted excitedly. The word Dana spoke to him flashed into his mind and he remembered that she said God would reveal what it meant to him.

"That's it, KT. The word that Dana told me was Oneness," he said excitedly. His brain was now ticking over rapidly.

"The people are one and they all have one language. Now nothing they propose to do will be withheld from them. That's it!" he repeated.

"What's it?" KT hadn't got the revelation yet.

"I believe that's the key to unlock the problems in merged companies. Oneness. We need to get to the place where the two companies don't just merge but they truly become one and everyone is speaking the same language, so that nothing they plan to do will be impossible."

KT then got it. "The power of agreement."

Daniel hugged her tightly and she could tell he was fighting his emotions. When he pulled back a few moments later, his eyes were moist and he said in a hushed voice: "I can't believe that God spoke to me KT. He revealed what oneness means just as Dana said he would. God is amazing!"

KT was overjoyed for Daniel as she watched the dawning awareness on his face at the thought that the God he never really cared about before would care enough about him to give someone a word of encouragement for him, and then prove it by giving him the revelation he had promised. She was even more delighted to hear him acknowledge that God was amazing. Maybe there was hope for them.

26

On Saturday afternoon Daniel was torn. He didn't want KT to go but he was also consumed with the concept of oneness and wanted time to explore it further. He was eager to start developing strategies to create oneness in companies. He had read through the story in Genesis and he wanted to study it more thoroughly and hopefully get some more revelation. The fact that his dream had been on a construction site but he didn't recognize the structure that was being built was puzzling until he Googled 'Tower of Babel' and the diagrams of it resembled the structure he had seen in his dream. That blew him away! He had excitedly called KT to his laptop and showed her the weird tower.

Now they were at the airport and KT and the others had checked their luggage and were making their way towards the departure lounge. Just before they got to the security checkpoint, Paul shook Daniel's hand and said: "I'm glad I had this time to get to know you better. Let's catch up when you get back to Manhattan." KT noticed a look in Paul's eyes, almost as if he was reassuring Daniel which didn't make any sense to her. Daniel hugged Michaela who said, "Thanks so much for having us Daniel. We had a wonderful time. When you get back you'll have to come over for dinner."

"That would be great Michaela and any time you guys want to use the condo, just let me know."

They walked through security to give KT and Daniel some privacy. Daniel took both of KT's hands in his and looked her deeply in the eyes.

"I love you KT," he said.

She caught her breath. That was totally unexpected. Tears pooled in her eyes and spilled from her lower lids.

"Don't cry," said Daniel pulling her into his arms.

"Oh Daniel, I love you so much."

"I'm relieved! I thought you were crying because you had to tell me that you didn't love me," he teased.

She sniffed and smiled tremulously.

"Sorry that this isn't a more romantic setting but I couldn't keep it any longer."

"The setting is perfect," KT assured him. Having Daniel actually say that he loved her made any setting perfect.

He slid his hands into her hair and held her head in place as he kissed her deeply. "I'm going to miss you so much," he said huskily, pulling her in for one more hug. "I'll see you in a few weeks but I'll call you every day."

"That will cost a fortune," she protested.

"You're worth more than a fortune to me, KT."

"I'd better go before I start bawling," she sniffed.

229

They released each other with great reluctance and KT quickly walked away to give her passport to the security officer. She briefly turned around and waved as she got to the departure door, looking as if she would burst into tears at any moment. Daniel felt as if a part of him was leaving with KT and he wondered how he would get through the next five weeks.

Back at his condo Daniel felt incredibly lonely. The place seemed so empty and lifeless without KT. All he could do to ease the aching loneliness was to lose himself in his search to understand oneness which was beginning to obsess him. He turned on his laptop and went to get his copy of *Built to Last* while he waited for it to boot up.

Now that he'd discovered the concept of oneness, he was seeing it in the books he had brought. In the same story that he had discussed with KT about Team Guatemala in *Presence*, he recognized that when the team came into agreement, or oneness, things began to happen which had seemed impossible before, given the enmity that existed between them during the civil war. He also saw it in *Built to Last* where companies which had been around for a hundred years seemed to have succeeded in part because they indoctrinated newcomers into the culture, so that everyone spoke the same language and they were constantly sharing their vision so that everyone understood what they were aiming for and were committed to working together to achieve it.

Finally all the programs had been loaded and Daniel was able to open Word, start a new document and begin to type.

That night Daniel lay on his bed and waited for KT to call. She'd promised to call him when she got home which he expected would be about 10.30 p.m. her time or 11.30 in Barbados. While waiting he began to read Luke which he hadn't done much of since KT and the others were there. He soon began to see a pattern emerging. Jesus would teach the people and then he would do miracles. Daniel realized that he would communicate his message then he would demonstrate it. People began to follow him because they not only heard his message but they could see the truth of it being worked out before their eyes and they saw how it could benefit their lives.

He was still engrossed in his research when the telephone rang but he picked it up right away.

"Hello?"

"Hi Daniel. I've reached home safely. It's freezing here and I miss you already. But I just wanted to say thank you so much for what was the best week of my life."

"You're very welcome, KT and it's been the best week of my life too. The place is so quiet and empty without you. The only good thing is that I'm getting quite a lot of work done without you to distract me," he teased. "Maybe I'll come home earlier."

"That would be wonderful Daniel."

"I'll let you know. Glad you got back safely. Love you."

"Love you too. Bye."

Daniel hoped that she would still love him after he told her the truth. Maybe it was best not to say anything. Why spoil something this good? *The truth will set you free.* OK, roger that!

27

Three weeks later, Daniel walked into his apartment just before 11 p.m. and dropped his suitcase and laptop case next to the hall table. Barbados was wonderful but it was great to be home. At least he was in the same country as KT again. He'd planned to stay for the whole time but Bryan had called him a couple a days of ago to tell him that things were looking bad and that he should come back sooner rather than later. What he found amazing was his response to the situation. A year ago he would have been going crazy with worry, but for some reason he didn't feel worried. He felt that everything would be alright. He had a peace that he couldn't explain given the circumstances; it made no sense but it kept him sane.

He'd got a lot done and he'd managed to come up with several strategies to help merged companies, or those thinking about merging, based on the concept of oneness. When he took a break from working, he'd met Mandy's parents and had dinner out with the family one night. They seemed pretty reserved, at least compared to Mandy, but he put it down to their being English. He was glad that he and Mandy had agreed to be friends and he was truthful when he told her that he hoped to see her again sometime and wished her well with chef school.

Although he'd been fed on the plane, that seemed like hours ago and he was beginning to feel hungry. His throat also felt dry and a bit sore. Heading to the kitchen to see if there was anything edible in it, he was pleasantly surprised to find his fridge well stocked. He smiled and silently blessed Margaret for her thoughtfulness. When they got through this recession he'd give her a big raise. He made himself a sandwich, grabbed a coke and headed back to the living room where he sat on the couch and turned on the TV to see what was happening in the business news. It was much too late to call KT so he sent her a text just to let her know he was back in town.

That brought back the nagging question that followed him all the way from Barbados, kept him company on the plane, and now was here as well. Where, when and how would he tell KT about Mandy? He didn't want to tell her somewhere publicly so he'd either invite her here or go to her place. When? As soon as possible because it was eating him up. How? Well, he'd have to play that one by ear.

He'd bought her a bracelet at the airport in Barbados which he was eager to give her. He knew that she would think the gift was a bribe when he told her about Mandy but it wasn't. As soon as he saw the diamond and ruby bracelet he'd thought of KT and bought it for her. They might be in a recession but he wasn't destitute yet. Most women would be delighted with a gift like that but he'd probably have to persuade

KT to accept it. He'd have preferred to buy an engagement ring but he felt that would have been a bit presumptuous under the circumstances.

Suddenly feeling very tired and achy, he stood up, stretched and yawned and headed to the bathroom for a quick shower before bed. Tomorrow was another day.

Daniel awoke to the sound of the phone ringing next to his bed. He thought that he was dreaming for a while until the persistent ringing penetrated the fog of his sleep.

"Hello?" he managed in a hoarse voice. His throat felt dry and his body felt sore. He hoped he wasn't coming down with anything.

"Daniel I'm sorry if I woke you!"

"Hi KT, no problem, I don't mind you waking me up. In fact, I'd like you to wake me up every morning but with kisses."

"Daniel Tennant! I'm so glad you're back. I missed you so much."

"Me too. I wanted to see you today. I have a present for you but I feel as if I'm coming down with something and I wouldn't want to make you sick."

"Daniel, I work in a hospital, I'm not going to get sick. I can come around and bring you some chicken soup as soon as I can. Would that be OK?"

"I'd love you to KT if you're sure you'll be alright. My apartment is Penthouse 2 in the East River Apts on 59th Street. There's underground parking. Can't wait to see you."

Daniel's heart accelerated at the thought of KT coming to his apartment. He wasn't sure if it was excitement because he hadn't seen her for three weeks or if it was anxiety at having the opportunity to tell her about Mandy. Was this really the best time? He dragged himself to the bathroom feeling a bit weak and slightly feverish. This was not how he envisaged entertaining KT in his penthouse but maybe she'd be more sympathetic to him in his illness. He hoped so.

KT rang the doorbell to Daniel's apartment. She'd gotten a bit lost on the way but she was here at last. She looked around appreciatively while she waited for Daniel to open the door. Only the best for Daniel, she thought as she looked at the luxurious foyer and then remembered the vow he had made to never lack for anything again.

Daniel opened the door dressed in black silk pajamas. His hair was mussed up and he looked as if he'd just gotten out of bed. He was gorgeous. He held the door open and KT walked into his arms carefully balancing the bowl of chicken soup she had managed to make. Daniel held her tightly, almost desperately, even as he said: "I hope you don't get sick."

"I'll be fine," she insisted. "Now show me the kitchen and you go and lie down. I'll take care of you."

Daniel showed her the way to the kitchen and headed back to bed. He could get used to this, even if he was too ill to fully enjoy it right now.

A few minutes later KT came in with a bowl of soup which she put on the bedside table to cool. She pushed back Daniel's hair and felt his brow which was a bit warm.

"You feel feverish. Do you have a thermometer?"

"No, I don't think so. I've got some tablets in the cupboard in my bathroom if you don't mind getting a couple for me."

"No problem." KT passed through the walk-in closet and went into the bathroom to look for the medicine. The bathroom was very masculine and sophisticated, decorated in creams and dark blues with gold plated faucets. It was kind of strange being in Daniel's space, seeing his shaving stuff, his cologne etc but it felt intimate and she liked it. Finding the tablets in a small medicine cabinet she took them to him and went to the kitchen to get a glass of water.

"You didn't have to bring me soup you know KT, but I really appreciate it. I love having you here."

"I love being here," she admitted feeding him some soup "and I know you're too weak to try anything." He laughed ruefully well aware that she was right about that.

"Oh, I almost forgot. I brought you a present. It's in my laptop case near the front door. Would you mind bringing it? Sorry to give you all this work."

"You bought me a present? Oh Daniel, you didn't have to!" She found his laptop bag dropped on the floor next to his suitcase and took it to him. Daniel removed a bag from it and took out a square but flattish box which he held back for a moment.

"When I saw this at the airport I immediately thought of you so I hope you like it and that you'll accept it." He handed her the box keeping his eyes on her face.

KT opened the box and put a hand over her mouth which had dropped open. Her eyes immediately filled with tears. "Daniel this is beautiful!" she struggled to control her tears. "You're not going to believe this but when we were leaving Barbados I walked into a store at the airport and saw this very bracelet and admired it but I couldn't afford it. How did you know?"

"I didn't know. Maybe it's a sign." KT hugged him and let him put on the bracelet for her.

"Thank you Daniel. I'll treasure it."

Daniel knew it was now or never. "KT this is not how I intended to do this but I want you to know that I love you very much and I'm serious about you so I want us to go forward with a clean slate, no secrets between us." He paused. KT had a sudden feeling of disquiet as if she knew she wouldn't like what Daniel was about to say.

"I've changed a lot since I've come to know you KT and I really regret some of the things I did in the past. I wish I could go back and change them."

"The past is the past, Daniel, let's forget about it."

"I agree, but I need to tell you about something that happened when I was in Barbados." KT's heart felt as if it stopped and then started to race. Daniel looked at her remorsefully as he said: "Just before you agreed to come to Barbados, an English girl who was staying in one of the condos invited me over to dinner as a thank you for putting some sunscreen on her back." He could feel KT begin to withdraw even though she didn't physically move. He met her gaze bravely and pressed on: "One thing led to another and we ended up sleeping together."

KT stood up and backed away from the bed, clasping her hands around her waist as if she were in pain. Tears of anguish sprang to her eyes and rolled down her cheeks. She couldn't believe that Daniel would do such a thing and then invite her to come and visit. She wondered if she had walked past the woman, maybe even spoken to her not knowing that she and Daniel had slept together. The hurt that ripped through her was agonizing. How could Daniel do such a thing and then say that he loved her?

Daniel's heart tore at the pain he'd caused her. "I'm sorry, KT. It didn't mean anything. It was just physical. I even apologized to Mandy afterwards. I never meant to hurt you."

"You didn't think this would hurt me? For all I know I walked past this Mandy on the beach all during the holiday and never even knew that you slept with her. She must have been laughing behind my back."

"No, KT, she and her family were away for that week."

"Oh is that why you invited me? To have something to do while she was away?"

"Of course not KT! It wasn't like that. You're not being rational. I wanted you with me; I wanted to share Barbados with you. I want to share my life with you KT." He hadn't intended to say that but it just came out. He could see KT slipping away and he didn't want to lose her.

"Well I want no part of your life, Daniel Tennant, if sharing it means sharing you with every willing female."

"It doesn't, KT. I would never do that again."

"And how do I know that Daniel? How can I trust you again? I should have listened to the people who warned me to stay away from you. I can't deal with this right now. I have to go. Don't bother to get up, I'll let myself out." And with that she walked out. Daniel didn't try to stop her. He knew that she was hurt and he had to give her some time, but how much? If he thought he had felt bad the night he slept with Mandy it was nothing compared to the agony that was slicing through him now. Was this how his father felt when he wouldn't forgive him? He closed his eyes and said: "Jesus."

KT drove blindly to Desiree's apartment, wiping her eyes constantly as fresh tears coursed down her cheeks. She could see curious stares aimed at her as she stopped at traffic lights but she was too hurt to care. She eventually arrived at Des' place without wrecking the car.

Desiree answered the door after a couple of knocks.

"Hi, KT," she started out cheerfully and broke off abruptly as KT burst into tears again.

"What's happened?" she asked anxiously, looking intently into her face.

"Daniel Tennant happened! Oh Des, everyone was right. He hasn't changed at all. He slept with someone in Barbados just before I went there!"

"Oh! The dog! How did you find out?"

"He told me just now. He said that it didn't mean anything and it was just physical. That doesn't make it hurt any less. I feel so betrayed! After the wonderful week we spent together and him telling me that he loved me at the airport, I feel so stupid and so deceived."

"Oh, KT, I'm so sorry. It probably really didn't mean anything to him, given his previous lifestyle. You realize that he didn't have to tell you and you would never have known? So maybe he does care about you and just wants to go forward without any secrets."

"That's what he said, but I can't deal with him right now."

"Give it some time," suggested Des. "If you and Daniel are meant to be together God will work it out."

## 28

*New York Times June 18, 2009*
*Tennant Consulting lands historic merger*

*Tennant Consulting has just signed a contract to be the consultant in the Biomass/Solar Farm merger, the largest merger of biotechnology companies to date in the US. The fact that the merger market has declined during the recession must make closing this deal even sweeter for Tennant Consulting.*

*There is also talk that a new consulting division in Tennant's company, will assist with the post-merger integration. This is in stark contrast to the "Love 'em and leave 'em" philosophy of Tennant, who, until fairly recently, was well known for assisting with mergers, walking away with a fat check and not looking back...*

Daniel grimaced to himself as he leaned back in his chair. He put down the New York Times and looked out of the window of his office, absently noticing that many of the windows in the nearby buildings were now darkened. Glancing at his watch he saw that it was after

8:00 p.m. He'd been working long hours ever since he came back to work just over two months ago but there was nothing to go home to and he hardly went out any more so what else was there to do?

He glanced at the article again. "Love 'em and leave 'em?" Yes that was him less than a year ago. He could remember some of the things he'd done both in business and in his personal life. Things that now made his stomach turn. No wonder people were still so skeptical about this turnaround in him. The episode with Mandy in Barbados still sickened him and what made it worse was the fact that KT had not spoken to him since that day in his apartment. He'd tried to call her several times and at first she just ignored his calls then one day she actually answered but it was just to tell him that she wasn't ready to talk with him just yet. It was frustrating and agonizing that he couldn't be with her and show her how much he'd changed, but he knew that he had to give her some space. He had told her that patience was one of his virtues but trying to be patient about this was nearly killing him.

His PR firm had booked him to do an interview on The Beacon Live to promote the new business division and he'd agreed because he really believed that the concept of oneness was the key to success in business. He needed to leave now if he was going to get home to pack and get some sleep before his early morning flight to Atlanta. No doubt Jason Beacon, The Beacon as he was known on TV, would bring up his past just to boost the show's ratings. Everyone liked a bit of dirt and there probably wasn't a bigger skeptic alive on Prime Time TV.

Daniel stood up and stretched. Throwing a few files into his briefcase and picking up his laptop bag, he turned off the light and left his office. The elevator took him swiftly to the basement garage where his Porsche was parked. Triggering the keyless entry, he opened the door and slung his bags on the passenger seat and climbed in, starting the powerful engine. The power of the engine gave him the usual rush and he was sorry that he didn't have time to go for a spin outside the confines of the city. He was tired though. He was tired from the long hours that he had been putting in since KT left his apartment, but he was also tired of the newspapers invading his privacy, and tired of his past always being resurrected.

The nasty letter he'd received yesterday didn't help either. It was from a former client, Patterson Morgan, who was very happy with his merger when it was finished three years ago but who was blaming him now that it wasn't working out. It wasn't the first such letter he'd gotten and it probably wouldn't be the last. People tended to get that way when they saw that the millions they spent to acquire another company weren't paying off the way they'd expected. He'd give him a call when he got back in town and see if his new division could help if things were not too far gone.

He made a mental note of it as he drove towards his apartment. His thoughts returned to the New York Times article. That person no longer existed. He did things differently now. People could change. He grimaced as he remembered the conversation he'd had with KT almost a year ago when he told her that he didn't believe that people could change. The mere fact that he'd been celibate for about four months now was proof. Of course to date four months was his limit so he couldn't get too comfortable. Apart from that fiasco with Mandy, he could hardly remember a time before his surgery when he wasn't sleeping with someone or the other but he no longer led that lifestyle and he was doing OK. Well barely, he admitted. He thanked God for Margaret and Bob who really encouraged him to stick to his new path and who held him accountable.

He turned on the radio to listen to some music just as the radio host was introducing some band called Flyleaf which he'd never heard of. What kind of a name was Flyleaf anyway? He left it on and let the lyrics wash over him…

All my complaints shrink to nothing
I'm ashamed of all my somethings
She's glad for one day of comfort
Only because she has suffered

Fully alive
More than most

Ready to smile and love life
Fully alive and she knows
How to believe in futures…


He could relate to some of that. He had to admit that he was ashamed of all his "somethings", but he had suffered a lot this last year, physically and emotionally, and had come out alive. He wasn't fully alive though, not since KT had walked out, but while his personal life was in shambles, at least he was excited about his work again and it wasn't just about the money anymore. His pleasure was now from trying to figure out how to help newly merged clients through that difficult post-integration phase.

They may still refer to him as the Merger Mogul in the media - the hard, ruthless, determined consultant who made sure his clients got the target they wanted at the best possible price – but he had changed. In the past he did what he had to do to make sure that his client got the company they were going after if he considered it a good fit and at the best possible price. That was his job and he did it well. Now he was committed to not only bringing companies together, if that's what they wanted, but helping them to stay together. He only wished he was as successful doing that in his own life with KT.

He was still in contact with Paul who'd told him that KT wasn't seeing anyone and he was pretty sure that she still loved him and to give her some more time. He'd invited him to his and Michaela's fifth wedding anniversary lunch on Sunday and KT would be there. He hoped that he'd have the opportunity to speak to her alone.

"Caveat Emptor! Let the buyer beware." The words dropped from Jason Beacon's lips with just a hint of a smile. "That's what you were reported to have said after the collapse of Shellbury almost a year ago when their merger failed." He picked up a photocopy of the old Wall Street Journal article and read: Merger Mogul, Daniel Tennant, says: "People don't usually go into marriage expecting to get divorced, but divorce happens. That's why people should protect themselves with a prenupt. In the world of M&A's there are no prenupts and no guarantees. When I'm the consultant in a merger I do everything to make sure that the fit is right and I try to leave no stone unturned in the due diligence but no deal is perfect and we have little control over what happens afterwards. Caveat Emptor!"

JB: Were you implying that Barton Phillips, who was the consultant on that merger, didn't do his homework properly?

So this is how it's going to be, thought Daniel, attack up front. He gave a brief smile and said: "I would never speculate about another consultant's work. As I've said before, they're no guarantees with mergers.

Getting together is one thing, living together is another thing. However, what I'm trying to do now, that I didn't do before, is help my clients get through the honeymoon period."

JB: What's changed? What made you set up your new division of Tennant Consulting? For those of you who don't know what's been happening in the M&A world, Tennant Consulting in the last few months has set up a new division to hold the hands of their clients through the post-merger issues. To quote yesterday's New York Times "This is in stark contrast to your "Love 'em and leave 'em" philosophy of the past." What changed?

Daniel: Well, JB, I changed. The way I looked at things changed and those changes caused me to want to operate differently. In addition to that, we all know that the M&A market can be cyclical based on recessions, so I felt that we needed to diversify so that all of our eggs weren't in one basket.

KT's phone rang just as she was washing her dinner dishes. She quickly dried her hands and ran to the cordless phone which was on her coffee table.

"Hello."

"KT, is your TV on?" asked Des excitedly.

"No, why? What's happened?"

"Turn on The Beacon Live. Daniel's on."

KT automatically picked up the remote, turned on the TV and scrolled through the channels until she came to The Beacon Live. She just couldn't help herself.

"I'll call you back Des," she said vaguely.

She hungrily devoured Daniel on the screen. She hadn't seen him since the day she left his apartment and she noticed that he looked as if he'd lost a little weight but he was still so handsome. She sat down and turned up the volume.

JB: Well you know that nothing is private for celebrities like yourself, so we understand that you had a near-death experience and that shook you up. Is that true?

Daniel: I'd hardly call myself a celebrity, but yes that is exactly what happened. Last September I discovered that I had a brain tumor. Fortunately, it was operable but it gave me a wakeup call and caused me to begin to re-examine my life. I spent several months in recovery which allowed me a lot of time to think about my life, the meaning of it, or if, in fact, it had any meaning. I realized that I didn't like what I saw so that was the kick in the butt I needed to snap out of my purposeless existence and change my lifestyle.

JB: Putting together multi-million dollar mergers can hardly be considered purposeless.

Daniel: What does it mean if you gain the whole world and lose your soul? I was losing my soul.

JB: So you're telling us that your approach to business and in fact life in general has drastically changed? Is the fact that you're never seen out on the town with beautiful women anymore part of that change?

Daniel: Yes. I made some bad choices and hurt someone that I care about deeply. Nothing was worth that.

Tears sprang to KT's eyes and the ice around her heart melted as she heard Daniel's words spoken publicly and sincerely. Who was she to be unforgiving when she'd been forgiven so much? She felt deeply ashamed that she had let her feelings of hurt override her love and compassion for Daniel when she knew that he wouldn't have had the strength to resist the temptation on his own.

JB: What's next? Will you be handing out tracts on the street corners of Manhattan?

Daniel (laughing): Not likely! I'd probably be carried off in a straight jacket.

JB: I'm not much of a believer that people can change. So I wonder how long this phase will last.

Daniel: We'll have to agree to disagree on that JB because it's not a phase for me. At 36 I'm too old for phases and too young for a mid-life crisis. I have some great people in my life who encourage me and who hold me accountable to the changes I've committed to.

JB: Sounds like AA. Maybe we should all get into some kind of group to keep us accountable. There definitely needs to be one for the brokers and mortgage dealers who offered credit to unqualified customers. So are you planning to retire as The Merger Mogul and focus on the post-merger side of things?

Daniel: I've been giving it some serious thought. In fact, as I see the number of mergers that are failing I'm beginning to wonder if mergers should happen in the first place.

JB: Why is that? Aren't they supposed to create synergies, streamline processes, access new markets, all of that good stuff?

Daniel: In theory, but what often happens is that the cultures of the two companies don't always gel and it can lead to sometimes insurmountable problems after the merger.

JB: So what can we look forward to from you in the future Daniel?

Daniel: Well, in my personal life, I would like to settle down soon. I'm not getting any younger and I have no heirs. In terms of business, I'm working on implementing oneness in companies. I got a revelation of that concept when I was recuperating in Barbados and it confirms something that the physicist David Bohm said which I read recently. He said: "The most important thing going forward is to break the boundaries between people so we can operate as a single intelligence." When we can begin to operate as a single intelligence in our companies, then I believe that we will be able to attain the success that we all desire and seem to fall so short of with only a few exceptions.

JB: Sounds interesting. Maybe when you get that working you can come back and talk to us some more. Daniel, thanks for coming and talking to us tonight.

Daniel: Thanks for having me JB.

JB: Well folks that was Daniel Tennant, The Merger Mogul, saying that he is ready to lose that title. And ladies, he's also looking to lose the title of Bachelor…

Oh, he was, was he? KT fumed. Was he seeing someone? Maybe he wasn't talking about her when he'd said that he hurt someone. She was confused; she didn't know what to think. What she did know though, was that she still loved Daniel. She'd never stopped.

## 29

Daniel found the address that Paul had texted him but, because he was so late, he had to drive past it to find a place to park. He noticed KT's car parked in the long driveway and was glad that she was here already because he figured that if she'd come and seen his car she may have left. It was Paul and Michaela's anniversary and all of their close friends and family would be there. He was looking forward to meeting KT's parents and her younger sister. He wondered if they knew anything about him. He hoped not. Taking the gift that Margaret had bought and put in the trunk of his car on Friday, he got out, braced himself and walked up to the front door. Paul opened the door and welcomed him inside.

"Hi Daniel, glad you could make it," he said shaking hands and clapping Daniel on the shoulder.

"Daniel, welcome!" Michaela added joining them.

"Hi guys. Happy anniversary," he replied offering the gift to Michaela with a kiss.

"Thank you Daniel. How are you doing? You look as if you've lost a little weight," she said in her direct way.

"I'm OK just working too many long hours."

"I know how that goes," agreed Paul.

"KT's here but she doesn't know we invited you," warned Michaela.

"I just hope she doesn't kill me when she finds out," teased Paul. "Let's go and face the music and I'll introduce you to my parents." He led the way to a large wooden deck at the back of the house. In the distance Paul could see a pool partially hidden behind some bushes. It was a beautiful property.

"You've got a great place here Paul," he said scanning the faces for KT's. He didn't know if to be disappointed or relieved when he didn't see hers.

"Thanks. We bought it recently at quite a steal in anticipation of children. I don't know where KT is, probably in the kitchen helping to organize the caterers or something. She and Val, my other sister, insisted that Michaela should do nothing today. My parents are over here." He led Daniel towards an attractive, interracial couple. KT's dad was tall and several shades darker than Paul and KT while her mum was no more that 5'4" and was a beautiful and elegant blond, whose hair was well maintained and expertly colored to conceal any gray.

"Mum, dad, this is Daniel Tennant, KT's friend and now mine, who we stayed with in Barbados. Daniel, my parents, Robert and Barbara Taylor."

"Mr. and Mrs. Taylor I'm so glad to meet you," and he wasn't being polite. He had looked forward to meeting KT's parents. "I can see where KT got her beauty Mrs. Taylor, but she told me that she didn't get your cooking genes."

Mrs. Taylor laughed. "I can't believe KT told you that she can't cook! Doesn't she know that the way to a man's heart is still through his stomach?" she teased.

"Well she's already got my heart, even if she can't cook," Daniel said honestly. KT's mum assessed him with fresh eyes and her dad said:

"Daniel Tennant. The Merger Mogul." Oh no, thought Daniel, what has he heard about me? "I saw you on The Beacon a couple of nights ago. I'm a retired banker but I still like to keep abreast of what's happening in business. I'd be very interested in hearing more about this "oneness" concept that you're talking about. Sounds like something a lot of companies could use."

"I'd be happy to get together with you some time to talk about it, sir," Daniel replied, relieved.

"Call me Robert."

"And I'm Barbara," his wife added.

"Thank you. I was just telling Paul what a beautiful property he has here," Daniel started to say when he noticed that something had caught the attention of the three Taylors. He turned to see that KT was walking from the house speaking to someone just behind her.

She turned around fully and stopped in mid-sentence as she saw Daniel. Her heart began to race.

"What are you doing here?" she asked abruptly. Daniel was the last person she expected to see there and she wasn't prepared for it.

"KT!" her mother scolded at her rudeness, looking somewhat shocked.

"Hello KT, I'm fine, thank you and how are you doing?" Daniel used her exact words to remind her of the time he'd called her apartment and Paul had answered the phone. Daniel was surprised that his voice sounded so calm because he was almost floored by how beautiful KT looked, even though slightly thinner, in an olive and black silk dress draped in some sophisticated style around her body and her hair loose about her shoulders. He wanted to bury his face in it and be enveloped with the fragrance of vanilla. He felt such a surge of love and desire for her that he had to struggle to restrain himself from taking her in his arms right there and then.

KT felt a reluctant smile tug at her lips. "Touché," she said totally unaware of the struggle going on inside Daniel. She was too busy trying to control the emotions coursing through her and to kill the desire to throw herself into his arms.

"Can we talk?" Daniel asked. They only had eyes for each other. KT's parents looked at them and then at Paul with questions in their eyes. Paul gave a slight shake of his head as if to say "Don't ask".

"OK, we can walk over by the pool."

"Excuse us," Daniel said and followed her down the stairs and over to the pool. KT sat on a lounge chair out of sight from the deck and Daniel pulled another one a bit closer and sat facing her.

"How have you been?" Daniel asked her.

"I've been better," KT admitted.

Daniel came straight to the point. "KT, I can't tell you how sorry I am about what happened in Barbados. I was serious when I said that it didn't mean anything. In fact, I felt so sick afterwards that I went back to my condo and picked up the Bible you gave me and started reading John, hoping it would make me feel better but it just exposed my sin. That's when I realized that trying to do things on my own wasn't working and I needed God's help to change, so I asked him to help me and he has been ever since. I know I don't deserve it but can you ever forgive me?" A picture of his father flashed into his mind and with it brought a feeling of shame that *he* had refused to forgive him when he had the chance and regret that it was now too late.

"None of us deserve it, but God forgives us, so how can I do any less? I'm glad that you're trying to do things his way now. You're finally free from the Matrix." She threw her arms around him in a hug. Pulling away she asked: "Did you mean what you said on The Beacon the other night? That nothing was worth hurting someone you cared about deeply? Did you mean me?"

"Of course I meant you KT. I love you and I want to be with you again."

"I forgive you, Daniel but I need some time to trust you again. I'm not quite ready to make any commitments just yet."

"I can live with that. So you're willing to give me another chance?"

"I am."

Daniel stood and pulled KT up to stand in front of him. With great restraint he kissed her forehead and then took her hand to walk back to the party. KT felt disappointed that he hadn't kissed her properly. What was wrong with her? First she told him she needed time and then she was sorry that he was taking his time. She must be bipolar.

"I like your parents," Daniel said as they walked.

"I'm sure they like you as well. You're nothing if not charming when you want to be. So I understand that you're planning to give up the title of Bachelor?" she teased not quite sure how she felt about that. "The single women will probably be coming out of the woodwork now."

"I've only got eyes for one," he said seriously looking at her. KT smiled and continued walking. It felt so good being with Daniel again.

The day took on new color for Daniel and KT. KT introduced him to her baby sister, Valerie. She was several inches shorter than KT, had her dad's coloring and wore her hair in a natural curly style. She whispered rather loudly to KT that Daniel was "hot" which made him laugh and give her a hug. Then he met Michaela's parents and their friends. The buffet put on by the caterers was wonderful but Daniel couldn't remember what he ate, he was so busy devouring KT with his eyes. Eventually KT's dad pulled him away for a "talk" he said. Daniel thought he'd wanted to talk about "oneness" and was surprised when he said: "Young man, I can't help but notice that you can't take your eyes off my daughter and I was just wondering what your intentions are or if I'll have to get out my shotgun."

Daniel laughed and said: "You won't need a shotgun, Robert, unless it's to convince KT to marry me. I love her and I'm trying to convince her to spend the rest of her life with me, if we have your blessing."

"And why would she need convincing of that?"

"It's a long story and not very pretty. Suffice it to say I betrayed her trust but I'm happy that she's forgiven me and I won't let her down again, with God's help."

"Well that's good enough for me."

"Thank you, sir."

"What are you two talking about?" asked KT walking up to them.

"Oh, men stuff," said her father putting his arm around her shoulder and giving her a quick hug. "I like this young man. Don't keep him in suspense for too long," he said heading back to the party.

"Now you've got my whole family on your side," complained KT.

"When I'm preparing for a merger, I pull out all the stops. And this is the most important merger of my life. I can't afford to mess it up."

"OK Mogul." Daniel laughed and gave KT a quick hug.

"I think it's time I was leaving. Are you ready to go? I can drive behind you to make sure you get home safely."

"Thanks Daniel but I'll be fine."

"When can I see you again? Would you like to go to a show this week?"

"I'd love to. Mama Mia has just started and I would love to see that."

"OK, Mama Mia it is. I'll get Margaret to book some tickets and I'll call you and let you know what day."

"Great! See you then." Daniel said his goodbyes to everyone and made his way to his car. For the first time since KT walked out of his apartment he felt fully alive.

"Thank you Lord," he said out loud.

30

The first thing Daniel did when he got to his office on Monday morning was deal with the letter from Patterson Morgan. Daniel had worked on the merger between Morgan's financial services firm and a similar firm which offered specialist services. The merger had gone well and everyone had been happy, Daniel included, especially when he walked away with a big check.

Unfortunately according to Morgan's letter, cracks were not just beginning to show but they seemed to be threatening the whole structure and he obviously wanted a scapegoat. Daniel supposed the most convenient one was Tennant Consulting.

He thought that this would be a perfect opportunity to test his oneness strategy and smooth things over with Patterson Morgan at the same time. He reached for the phone on his desk.

"Margaret, get me Patterson Morgan at Morgan Stanley please."

"Sure Daniel." A minute later his phone rang.

"Hello Patterson. I got your letter last week but I've been out of town so I wasn't able to deal with it. I'm sorry to hear that things are bad over there but I may be able to help. I've got a new strategy that I'm offering to help companies with their post merger issues. How would you like to get together this week to discuss it?

After agreeing a date and time, Daniel hung up satisfied with the call. Maybe that letter that had seemed so threatening was really a blessing in disguise.

Daniel lavished attention on KT as he had never done with any other woman. He arrived to pick her up for Mama Mia with a single rose the exact color of the dress she wore on their first date.

"I'll never forget our first date and the color of the dress you wore," he said handing her the rose. KT was touched that he remembered her dress after all these months however she preferred not to remember how the date ended.

One weekend he picked her up and let her drive his Porsche down to Long Island where they had a picnic. "You know a man must really be in love when he lets a woman drive his Porsche," he joked. KT laughed as she felt the power of the engine respond to the slight increase in the pressure of her foot on the gas.

KT dragged Daniel to the cinema, something he hadn't done for years, to watch a romantic comedy.

"Admit it, you enjoyed it," she teased afterwards.

"Well the guy got the girl in the end so that gives me hope. But I still prefer Matrix."

"Typical male!"

He never made any attempt to do more than kiss her cheek or forehead and while it was almost killing him he felt it was the best way to regain her trust. KT enjoyed being with Daniel but she was also frustrated with the restraint he was showing. He would only hold her hand and kiss it or just brush his lips to her forehead when he left her at her door while she longed for him to kiss her with the passion that he had on their first date. In fact it seemed to her that he avoided lingering when he dropped her off. She began to wonder what his hurry was and if perhaps he was seeing someone else. Maybe someone who was giving him what she wasn't.

Daniel drove off after seeing KT to her door. He didn't dare stay any longer because it was becoming nearly impossible to keep his hands off her and give her those chaste kisses when he really longed to hold her close and indulge himself in the taste and feel of her as he did before. But that was just too much given his enforced celibacy. He said a quick prayer for strength. He needed to marry her soon.

It was KT's birthday, a warm night in August, when Daniel picked her up to take her to dinner.

265

"Happy Birthday," he greeted her at her door with a bouquet of colorful flowers and a beautifully wrapped gift.

"Thank you Daniel, these are beautiful. I'll just get a vase for them. And thank you for the gift; I'll open it in the car." KT was back in a couple of minutes. She found Daniel looking uncharacteristically restless and asked if he was OK.

"Yes, I'm fine. I've got a special evening planned and I hope you'll enjoy it."

"I'm sure I will. Where are we going? Tell me, don't make me wait!"

"I see that your patience hasn't improved," he laughed. "Well we're going to The Parisienne for dinner and then I've arranged for a carriage ride in Central Park."

"Oh, how romantic! I heard that the Parisienne is one of the most romantic restaurants in Manhattan and I've never been for a carriage ride in Central Park. And just to prove that I'm patient I won't open my gift until I get home."

Their dinner was wonderful. KT and Daniel reminisced about their first date which now seemed so long ago. She reminded him about the photo in the tabloids the next day and they laughed about it.

"I never did see that," Daniel said.

"Just as well. Paul called me up furious and read it to me. It said something like 'The Merger Mogul is back on the town and was seen at The Black Pearl with a mysterious Vanessa Williams lookalike...' That was rather flattering, I must admit."

"You're just as beautiful as Vanessa Williams and I'll never forget how stunning you looked that night. I totally lost my head."

"OK let's change the subject before I die of embarrassment."

They had dessert and then headed out to Central Park for their ride.

"Your carriage awaits, my lady," said Daniel helping her up into the carriage. The driver took off with a shake of the reigns.

"This is so beautiful," exclaimed KT as she admired the beauty and serenity of the park in the midst of all the high rises around it.

"*You* are so beautiful," murmured Daniel taking her hand. "KT, when I met you, your values seemed old-fashioned to me but, like this carriage ride, they are a refreshing reminder of the way things used to be. Thank you for coming into my life and introducing me to the real world."

"It was totally God, Daniel. But I'm glad he used me to reach you."

He reached into the pocket of his jacket which was next to him on the cushioned seat and took out a small black box. Flipping open the lid he revealed a princess cut diamond solitaire ring. KT put her hand over her mouth in awe. "You're like this diamond, rare and precious. Will you marry me and enter into a lifelong merger with me?"

"Yes, Daniel! I'll marry you." She threw her arms around him and he hugged her tightly, feeling as if he'd come home at last.

"This is so beautiful," she said in awe as he slipped the ring on her finger.

"When do you want to get married? I can't wait more than a couple of months. I feel as if I've been waiting for you forever."

"Let's get married in November. That will make a year that we first met. Can we get married in Barbados?"

"Are you sure you want to do that?"

"Absolutely! I love that island and I don't want the memory of it to be tainted by what happened there. I want our marriage and honeymoon to totally replace all the negative feelings with love and joy."

"Then Barbados it is. Let's go celebrate our engagement. I have a bottle of champagne at home in the fridge."

"Do you think that's a good idea?" asked KT. 'Don't go,' said a voice. 'You can trust him,' said another one. 'He's been the perfect gentleman.'

"You can trust me," Daniel said. "I know the boundaries."

"OK. In that case I'd love to have a glass of champagne to celebrate." She felt a tingle of excitement go through her body.

A similar excitement raced through Daniel and he wondered if he was tempting fate by inviting KT to his apartment. He knew the boundaries all right, but could he stay within them?

"I didn't really get to see your apartment last time I was here," KT reminded Daniel. He preferred to forget the outcome of that visit. "It's beautiful," she continued "but it's not terribly homey. It looks like a bachelor pad."

"It is a bachelor pad," laughed Daniel, "but you can make it as homey as you like when we get married. That is if you want to live here."

"I may have to exorcise the ghosts of girlfriends past," teased KT. Daniel wisely refrained from commenting and instead went to get the champagne.

"Here's to the most important merger of my life," he toasted and they touched their glasses together.

"And here's to the best merger specialist in Manhattan," she returned "who now not only brings the companies together but is committed to keeping them together." They drank their champagne and KT laughed in sheer happiness as the bubbles tickled her nose.

"I love you KT. Do you know that the first time I met you, I said to myself 'Kathryn Tennant sounds even better than Kathryn Taylor and you wouldn't even have to change your initials.'?"

"You did not!"

"Yes I did.  Maybe I had some kind of prophetic insight that we'd end up together."

"That's amazing.  I never would have guessed.  I thought you were pretty disgusting though."

"And I thought that you were from the Victorian era. I figured that you were prudish and a bit uptight but now I know that you just live by your principles and you're actually very warm and passionate."

"How would you know?  You haven't really kissed me in ages. I was beginning to think that you were seeing someone else."

"Seeing someone else?  Are you crazy?  I've been losing sleep trying to figure out ways to keep my hands off you."

"Oh. I'm so glad! Not that you've lost sleep but…" KT didn't finish her sentenced because Daniel pulled her onto his lap and began to kiss her with all the passion and love that he had stored up over the past months. She felt that she was being washed away by a torrent and all she could do was hold onto him for dear life.

Daniel's mouth left hers and trailed down her neck, tasting the skin as he went. KT threw back her head to give him better access and buried her fingers in his thick hair. He slid the zip of her dress down a few inches and bared her shoulder, continuing to nibble on her soft skin until she shuddered with pleasure. Daniel wanted nothing more than to lower the dress all the way and sample what she was willingly offering. She really didn't know what she was doing to him. She trusted him that he could stop before things went too far. She didn't know how wrong she was!

'Help me Lord, help me Lord,' he sent up a silent prayer. 'Give me the strength to stop. I don't want to fail you.' It was as if heaven was just waiting for him to ask for help because immediately he felt the power come over him to slide KT's zip up and pull away. He gathered her to him in a hug that was now free of passion but full of love. He slid her off his lap and leaned his forehead against hers, taking a ragged breath.

"Oh Daniel, I'm sorry! Sorry I led you on like that."

Daniel put his finger on her lips and said: "Don't apologize. I was with you all the way. But thankfully

God was with us as well and gave me the strength to stop.  I want our wedding night to be perfect, KT.  No regrets.  So let's do this God's way. OK?"  KT nodded.

"I love you Daniel.  Thank you for loving me enough to wait."

31

Daniel and KT flew down to Barbados in November with their closest friends and family to get married on the beach at Sandy Lane. KT's parents, Robert and Barbara were there, as well as Paul, Michaela and Val. Daniel arranged for Margaret, Bob and Des to fly in as well as Claire and Bryan from the firm. Bryan was Daniel's best man and Des was KT's maid of honor. As Daniel looked at their friends and family, he felt a pang of sorrow that his parents weren't alive to share this moment with them.

Claire came up to Daniel and said with a very serious expression: "Daniel do you have a prenupt?" Daniel looked at her in disbelief for a second before the pin dropped and he threw back his head and laughed as he remembered the day at the retreat when Claire had told him one day he would fall hard and be running to the altar to create his own merger without having a prenuptial agreement.

"OK, I admit it. I've lost it," he replied giving her a hug, "but it's great!" Claire laughed and said: "I told you so."

The beautiful ceremony was performed by a local minister against the backdrop of the most amazing sunset and afterwards the guests were treated to a sumptuous dinner and then dancing to the music of a Barbadian band. They finally said goodnight to their guests and were driven by limousine to Daniel's condo.

"That was the most perfect wedding," she declared settling back in the limo.

"That's because you were the most perfect bride."

"Flattery will get you everywhere," promised KT.

"And I can't wait," murmured Daniel kissing her at last with all the passion he had restrained over the last months.

"Are you sure you didn't want to stay at Sandy Lane tonight?" he asked opening the door to the condo. He picked her up and carried her over the threshold.

"Absolutely not! Do you know how many times I wished you didn't have to sleep on the couch when I was here? Now we can actually share your bed."

"KT, I'm glad that we did this God's way and waited until we got married. You are giving me a precious gift that very few women have to give their husbands and I will treasure it."

"Thank you Daniel. I'll go and get ready for you."

Daniel showered in the guest bathroom and was lying in his bed in his robe when KT walked out of the dressing room draped in a sheer white nightgown. Her hair was loose down her back and she wore no make-up; to him she was the most beautiful woman he had ever seen and she was all his. He rose from the bed and walked over to her.

"You can't imagine how I've longed for this time. I'll try to make it perfect for you because you deserve nothing less."

"I don't care about perfection. I just want you."

"And I want you, desperately."

Daniel took KT in his arms and held her tightly. He knew that he had to restrain himself from rushing and he prayed for strength and restraint. At once he felt a peace and strength flow into him. He kissed KT gently, almost reverently, running his hands down her back over the silk of her nightgown. He slipped the straps over her shoulders, kissing each one in turn as the silk pooled at her feet.

"Perfection," he whispered. "You are fearfully and wonderfully made." He kissed the curve of her neck and her shoulders. "How beautiful you are, my darling! Oh, how beautiful!" Scripture verses were flowing from him that he didn't even know.

"How handsome you are, my lover!" she quoted in response feeling the strength of his back and shoulders.

He admired her beauty, caressing her body while murmuring the words of a traditional wedding vow: "With this ring I thee wed. With my body I thee

275

worship." Daniel carried her to the bed and began to worship her body with his. KT was enthralled by the beauty of their lovemaking and the feelings she was experiencing for the first time. Daniel encouraged her with words of praise and tender caresses until she was ready for him.

At the moment of the sealing of their marriage covenant, Daniel caught KT's brief cry in his mouth and held her close until she relaxed again.

"Thank you for your amazing gift" he murmured and began a rhythm as old as time.

A wave began to swell, pushing them steadily and unwaveringly towards a shore that they could feel getting closer and closer until it suddenly broke, tossing them into a maelstrom of intense pleasure and then slowly receding leaving them enveloped by a Presence so sweet, so holy that tears came to their eyes.

"I've never experienced anything like that," Daniel said softly when he was able to speak again.

"Neither have I," KT said in wonder, wiping her eyes. "It was as if God was here with us giving his approval."

*For this reason a man will leave his father and mother and be united to his wife and they will become one flesh.*

"We are now one," whispered Daniel.

## 32

*New York Times, November 15, 2010*
**Tennant Consulting Praised by Morgan Stanley**

*The Merger Mogul, Daniel Tennant, and Tennant Consulting have been praised by Patterson Morgan, CEO of Morgan Stanley, who attributes their two quarters of successive growth to the new Oneness Strategy that was implemented by Tennant Consulting at his company earlier this year. Morgan Stanley, which was on the brink of failure after a merger masterminded by Tennant himself four years ago, has shown a significant turnaround and looks set to continue that trend well into the future.*

*At the beginning of this year Tennant Consulting added another division to the firm bringing a new dimension to their consulting services. The division, which is jointly run by Tennant's wife, Kathryn and Business Coach, Karen Myers, focuses on team and relationship building in companies through activity based retreats and exercises…*

*One Week Later*

Daniel and KT sat on the set of The Beacon Live waiting for the cameras to roll. Daniel squeezed KT's hand reassuringly and brought it to his lips for a quick kiss. She smiled at him looking slightly nervous.

"You guys look like you're still on your honeymoon," quipped JB.

"It feels like we're still on our honeymoon," smiled KT.

"Well, Daniel, I think I'll have to eat my words. Last time you were here I said that I didn't believe people could change but you're living proof."

Before Daniel could reply the programme director called for silence and said: "We're going live in five, four, three, two, one."


JB: Good night everyone and welcome to The Beacon Live. Tonight our special guests are Daniel Tennant, aka The Merger Mogul, and his lovely wife Kathryn who everyone calls KT. Welcome Daniel and KT.

Daniel and KT: Thank you.

JB: Well Daniel it's been over a year since you were here. At that time you had just started talking about Oneness. What's been happening since then?

Daniel: Well my most successful Oneness project to date has been with my beautiful wife KT. We've been married for just over a year now and it's been amazing.

KT smiled at him radiantly.

JB: You're both obviously very happy together. I'm sure you're also happy to have KT working in the business. KT, I understand that you're a physiotherapist and in fact Daniel was your patient, that's how you met.

KT: That's right JB. After his surgery he was assigned to me for therapy but we didn't start to go out until after his treatments finished although he did try. (She laughed).

JB: What's it like working with Tennant Consulting especially since you've come from a background of working in a hospital?

KT: It's a great change and although I'm a part of Tennant Consulting I don't work there on a day-to-day basis, so I manage to keep out of Daniel's hair. My part of the business conducts retreats that focus on relationship building and team work through physical activities and exercises. Karen Myers, who is a Business Coach, brings the coaching dimension while I focus on the physical activities. That compliments the work that's being done in the other divisions of the firm.

JB: Daniel, Patterson Morgan, the CEO of Morgan Stanley attributes his firm's success to Tennant Consulting's new Oneness strategy. What do you say to that?

Daniel: Well I'm very glad that we could help Morgan Stanley. We were fortunate to have the team there very receptive to the strategies we suggested. Our role was to help them create a whole new entity with a new vision, a new culture and new values. We also worked with them on a communication strategy so that everyone was speaking the same language and through KT's and Karen's division they built inter-departmental relationships that were non-existent and were able to develop an understanding of how working together would help them to achieve the overall vision, even though each department also had its own goals to achieve.

JB: That sounds great but will it work in all companies?

Daniel: It has potential to work not only in all companies but in families, communities and even nations because it's based on principles, and principles are true wherever they are applied. The key is to apply them.

JB: Well you've heard it folks, Daniel Tennant, the Merger Mogul, and his beautiful wife, KT have been sharing their success with Oneness. Daniel or KT do you have any final comments?

Daniel: I've come to realize that many of the problems we face in the world today, not just in companies, are because we operate separately. It's me, my and mine and not we, our and ours. If we can get to a place where we operate as a "single intelligence" according to David Bohm, meaning that we operate as one and we also speak the same language, then nothing that we plan to do will be impossible for us.

*Three months later*


Daniel put down the New York Times as the phone on his desk rang.

"Daniel, there's a Ryan Thomas on Line one for you. He's calling from Barbados and he wants to talk to you about a project using your Oneness strategy."

"OK Margaret, I'll take the call." He pressed the button. "Daniel Tennant speaking."

"Hello Mr. Tennant, my name is Ryan Thomas. I'm the Chairman of the Strategic Planning Committee of the Ministry of Finance & Planning in Barbados. We've heard about the success you've been having using your Oneness strategy in companies and we understand that you believe it can work for nations as well. We're just a small nation but our vision is to make Barbados the number one place to live, work and do business and we would like you to work with us to get the whole nation on board to make it a reality. Is this something you'd be interested in and, if so, can you come to Barbados for an initial meeting?"

"It sounds like something I'd be very interested in. I'll have to check my schedule and let you know when I would be available. I believe that the principles we use will apply in any situation, but we have never done a nation before. It would definitely be a challenge if we decided to do it."

"If you give me your e-mail address I'll send a brief for you to look at. Then you can let me know about your availability and I'll set up a meeting between you, the Prime Minister and the rest of the Planning Team."

"That's fine. My e-mail is Daniel dot Tennant at Tennant Consulting dot com, all small letters. I'll read through the brief and get back to you." They exchanged goodbyes and Daniel hung up the phone with a look of amazement on his face. This was huge! He had the possibility of using Oneness to achieve something unheard of before – bring an entire nation together by sharing the same vision and speaking the same language so that they could achieve what would otherwise be impossible. That could only be God. He picked up the phone and pressed the intercom:

"Margaret, check my schedule for me and let me know if I have a few days free in the next couple of weeks. We may have to shift around some appointments. I need to fly to Barbados for a meeting with the Prime Minister. Margaret, I may have the opportunity to help transform an entire nation."

God can transform nations

Made in the USA
Charleston, SC
09 November 2012